Why is

Is it an
the drowning (or is it murder?) of a lady water taxi driver seventeen years ago in his teenage playground of Pittwater?

Has it something to do with a day lost to amnesia at that time?

Denny Traeger's shrink thinks so. So does a cold case detective he seeks out because of her knowledge of the suspected homicide.

Friction marks their investigating together. Worse, it prompts an assassination attempt on them both while up a creepy backwater. Ending in a fight for life and the gut-wrenching recall of the shocking event that caused his memory shutdown.

i

Also by Robin duMerrick

Sports Witch
Love Storm in Paradise
The Lady Could Kill for Love
Black Dog Cruise
Love Kills Twice
First Rays
Mock-A-Mate Lampoon Limericks

Robin duMerrick

Streaker

Streaker
By Robin duMerrick

#####

Published by ON Messij
Australia

Streaker
Copyright 2021 Robin duMerrick
ISBN: 978-0-6450729-1-4

This is a work of fiction. Names, characters, places and incidents either are the product of the author's imagination or are used fictitiously, and any resemblance to actual persons, living or dead, business establishments, events or locales, is entirely coincidental. Neither the author nor the publisher has any control over, and does not assume any responsibility for, third-party websites or their content.

Typeset in 11 pt Book Antiqua.

All rights reserved. Without limiting the rights under copyright reserved above, no part of this publication may be reproduced, stored in or introduced into a retrieval system, or transmitted, in any form, or by any means (electronic, mechanical, photocopying, recording or otherwise) without the prior written permission of the copyright owner and the publisher of this book.

"Living nude would be fine if it weren't for the five Ps: Prosecution, Protection from Prickles and the Perishing cold, and Pockets. That was a serious omission, not designing the human body with pockets."

Anon.

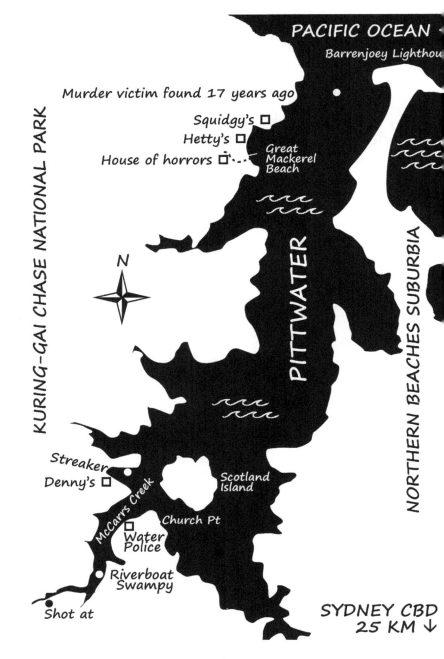

Streaker

1 : Bad choice

The boat sped south close to dark cliffs.

On this west side of five mile long Pittwater, the moon was the only light to pick up the boat's colour in the night. Pink. And the word spelt big on its sides. Taxi.

A world away, the distant eastern shore was a long humpback lit by a hundred thousand houses crawling over Barrenjoey Peninsular.

By contrast, the western shore was mostly wild. Backing it, endless acres of the Kuring-Gai Chase National Park. The only human habitation, a handful of small bays populated mostly by weekenders.

The northernmost bay was emerging now under the port bow of the water taxi. Great Mackerel Beach. A curve of sand between rocky headlands. An amphitheatre against brooding cliffs. A creek cutting a trickle trench across the sand near the farthest headland.

Cottages fringed the narrow beach. Halfway along, a jetty. One lamp on a pole at each end of the jetty. Another halfway along the walking track in front of the cottages.

Robin duMerrick

The only other light, a weak wash from a cottage deep into a gully on a track running away from the beach a few steps south of the jetty.

The engine growl eased as the boat rounded the south headland. Came off the plane. Ploughed to a walk, the sea reclaiming its calm. The new quiet disquieting.

The boat idled in under the end light of the jetty, revved briefly to nudge alongside. Which is when the lamp lit the occupants.

The driver, a woman in her late twenties. Slim, athletic. Untidy red hair. Behind her, two men. The tall one wiry, with black hair in a man-bun. His orange polo shirt and white tennis shorts neatly pressed. The short chubby man in a wrinkled Hawaiian shirt over bag-arsed jeans. An indulgent face.

The driver skipped from her helm seat to grab the jetty's rubbing strake and hold against the drift. The men stared at the stretching-out of her body. At what was in the denim shorts, whose leg hems were frayed way back beyond peekaboo bumcheeks, and almost backless top near the colour of her tan. Bare legs. Thongs on her feet.

The tall man jumped ashore with a case of beer. He waited for his companion to pay.

She held the rubbing strake with her left hand while her right took the banknote thumbed at her. She glanced at it. Pushed it back at the fat man.

"That's too much. Only thirty from Church Point to Mackerel. I told you."

"Keep it. Got to love that ass. You can take me for a ride any time, Toots."

She kept a straight face. Pointed to his wallet.

"You've got three tens there, I saw them."

"It's yours. Worth it for the peep show. See you, Toots. Next time it's you for me."

He lifted his own beer case, pretending not to see her

Streaker

nose wrinkle upward as if at a whiff of stomach gas. He stamped his foot on the seat and tried to make the step up manfully. Grunted as his bulk chose gravity over altitude.

Until the tall man leant in and laid a hand on the fat man's shoulder to heave him out. The manicured hand had a tattoo on its back. A crucifix with *Anesti* — "he rises" — under the icon.

The woman didn't move to help. She watched the circus blank-faced as she pocketed the bill.

"So you want me to pick you up after ...? What is it you're off to, anyway? The only lights in the bay don't look much like party lights."

The fat man made the jetty but seemed to have trouble straightening. He put down his beer case.

"You'd be surprised." He took a deep breath. "I'd invite you along, but I don't reckon it's your kind of party."

"You've got a mouth, Rollo, you know that? Why not shut it and let the lady go about her business?"

This one had a Canadian accent.

"Just making like social media live." The fat man not the least put out, believing in his charm offensive.

She not.

"Last chance. It's a long swim back."

"Another time, Toots. We're sweet for now. Drive safe."

"Yeah." Already moving to her swivel seat.

The two men watched the taxi head for the headland.

Until the tall man shouldered his beer case.

"Well, let's get to it. The others'll be along in a bit."

The two were halfway along the jetty before the tall man spoke again.

"If I didn't know you better, I'd think you liked lady meat."

3

Robin duMerrick

"The world's a smorgasbord, Vance. Gorge on it any way you can while you can, is what I say."

The engine buzz faded as the men dropped off the inland end of the jetty. The bay was left quiet. Just the lap of water on the rocks of the headland at the wake thrown up by the departing water taxi.

#

Cruising on Pittwater at night was the best of times. The spread of dash light wrapped the cockpit in a cocoon of light. Night's fingers clawed futilely at the driver just the other side of the windows.

Two different darks slid by. Close, the sea-black rippled with highlights from a cloud-shrouded moon. The backdrop, cliffs frowned, blacker still.

The engine's murmur comforted. The sea's hiss soothed. Ozone spun off wavelets' crests tantalised.

The driver grinned. Grinned wider when her eyes, checking the readings on the instrument panel, fell on the dog-eared photo stuck in a crack in the dash.

An eight year old boy and six year old girl straddling a paddle board, steadied by their mother standing, back to the camera, in the shallows of the surf's last gasp.

Happy days. More to come. Surely tomorrow, her day off.

Her eyes had barely returned to the dark ahead when the taxi lurched, its engine choked, coughed, choked again, died, and its hull, suddenly unpropelled, ploughed into the back of its own wake.

Silence.

"Oh, bugger."

She selected neutral, turned the ignition key. The engine came alive. She pushed into forward. A dull clunk shook the vessel and cut the engine.

"Don't tell me. Not twice in the same month."

A scowl uglied her almost pretty face. She worked the tilt on the control console at her right elbow. A servo

Streaker

whined, the outboard tilted its leg.

She swivelled her seat and paced to the stern. Stared. Grimaced. The propeller now clear of the water, wrapped in a tangle of orange rope.

She swore.

"I'll give Franco what-for when I see him. Him and his damn cray pots. Where'd I put that …?"

She rummaged for the knife in the stern locker. Thumbed the rusty blade. Wrinkled her nose. Glared at the tangle, gauging the rope by the thickness of her own little finger. Shook her head. Clambered out astern anyway and tried sawing at the fibres.

Swore again as a random slap of sea against hull had her hugging the engine cover to save herself from going overboard.

"Bugger." As she retreated to the cockpit. "Bugger, bugger, bugger."

Temper rose within her. She hurled the knife into the night.

She stood, fuming, hands on hips for half a minute, deep breathing easing her off the tantrum.

Eventually she had enough control to shrug and figure her options. She unshipped the paddle clipped under the port gunwale.

It was hard enough work to turn the boat. It would be harder to get the craft moving. Easier once she had way on. Still, a long haul back, even though she had not gone far from the southern headland into Mackerel.

"You party-heads better have a sharp something in your kitchen drawer."

She said it aloud. Under her breath she muttered her thanks that the slight breeze was with her not against her. Otherwise she didn't stand a chance.

#

She shipped her paddle as the taxi bumped the jetty. Leapt ashore and tied off. Turned to study the

Robin duMerrick

blue Caribbean 26 flybridge cruiser, with its twin 220 horsepower outboards, tied up on the opposite side.

She glanced at the name, Sappho, on the stern. Peered aboard into darkness.

"Hello there. Anyone aboard?"

No response. She shrugged. Trudged along the jetty.

At the land end, she paused. One walking track ran along the front of the cottages left and right. Another led inland up a shallow gully.

Her scan left and right confirmed that none of the waterfront weekenders was lit. Up the gully, it seemed, there was one, a brooding house set apart from the others on the right side of the grassy sloping ground.

She set off for it.

From a distance, it struck her as creepy enough. Worse as she got closer. Its front unlit. A faint light from the uphill side.

"Bates' Motel." She murmured her gold standard of creepy houses: the house by the motel in *Psycho*, the movie.

She mounted the veranda and knocked. Strained to hear if she'd been heard. Music so faint had her doubting her ears. Blinds pulled down on the front windows admitted no chink of light.

She cupped her face to peer into the sidelights either side of the front door. Still shadow shapes skulked against the dark. Nothing moved.

She came off the porch and went right, to the uphill side. Light came from a window toward the back. She approached. Peered in.

Shadows crawled over her face. Movement in the room. She frowned. Her face showed disbelief then horror.

Suddenly she staggered back, hand to mouth. Almost at once, a man's hand with a crucifix tattoo on

Streaker

its back clamped over her lips.

An arm around her waist pulled her back into the shadows.

#

Lit only by the dash light of the taxi, a manicured hand — on its back, a crucifix tattoo — got busy folding a tan halter-neck top onto thongs already neatly side by side on the helm seat.

The hand, making a "gimme" gesture to the thick shadow close by, prompted the sound of fabric slithering off flesh.

The sea gently slapped this hull and another.

"Come on. We don't have all day."

A chubbier hand came into the ambit of the pale light, holding frayed-hem denim shorts. Passed them into the manicured hands, which folded the denim on top of the shirt.

Another fingered "gimme" saw the pile topped by neatly folded pink panties.

"Awww. If only we had time for some necro." This from the dumpy shadow.

"You're a sick man, Rollo. Let's go. This one won't be the end of it." Then: "Did you get the rope off her prop?"

"Yep."

The two men bent. Grunted as they straightened and moved to the gunwale with their burden shared.

"Gently now. We don't want any bruises. She's supposed to've gone for a skinny-dip."

A woman's bare upper torso doubled over the gunwale, two silhouettes behind it. Hands lifted, letting it slip smoothly into the sea like a rehabilitated seal released. No splash.

The body bobbed, and settled, face down.

"Okay, let's get this thing towed away some. As if it drifted too far for her to get back on board."

Robin duMerrick

The silhouettes backed away. The taxi wobbled as the two men got off.

After seconds of silence, twin big outboards started in the near distance and idled off. The taxi jerked and slid aside, leaving black sea. The idling faded, leaving the lap of sea against body.

The body suddenly rolled over and unseeing eyes stared at the sky.

Streaker

2: 17 years later

Five nautical miles south of a murder at Mackerel Beach—and seventeen years after it—Denny Traeger stood at the end of a ferry wharf in Pittwater.

He was reading a folded newspaper, a briefcase at his feet. Dressed in an off-the-rack suit, no hat, sunglasses. Anyone watching would've pegged him as handsome, fit, serious, mid thirties.

He didn't look up at the chug of the small ferry that entered the deep narrow cove known as Elvina Bay and picked its way through the private yachts moored there.

From across the water, not quite masked by the beat of the diesel engine, Traeger heard yodelling.

The ferry's "toot" prompted him to raise his eyes. He glanced at his watch. Folded his paper. Unwrapped gum from his pocket. Chewed. Consulted his watch. Picked up his briefcase.

The chug slowed. The ferry, Pegasus, bumped alongside the jetty. The yodelling stopped. A skinny older man, hard-faced, drinking veins, with a white crew-cut, hustled from the wheelhouse. Stepped ashore with a breastline in his hands. Lassoed a jetty bollard with it.

Robin duMerrick

The older man had to raise his voice against the idling engine.

"Preggers lady this time, Mr Traeger. Sorry."

Denny Traeger grunted. Jumped aboard, sure-footed despite the bobble of the deck with the wake taking time to die. He dropped into the aft deck. Remained standing. Turned to pipe a peeved tone at the older man still on the Elvina ferry wharf.

"Third time this week, Yodel. I've got a meeting in town in thirty five minutes. How many pregnant women can you have on a commuter run, anyway?"

Grinning, Yodel flipped the loop off the bollard. Dropped the line along the gunwale. Pegasus began to drift under the light easterly. He sidled aft so he didn't have to shout. Ignored the drift.

"Not all preggers, Mr Traeger. Some pushin' prams. A few old dodderers. On the school run, young sprogs you can't trust to make the step aboard by theirself. I got to see to their safety even if it frigs with the timetable."

The younger man's eyes flicked left and right, gauging how long it would be before the drift took them into the nearest moored vessel, an ugly black-sided timber barge with nails as big as railway spikes canted loose along its rubbing strake.

"And I told you before to knock off the mister. Just Denny." Said absently.

"Denny, right? Not Danny. Yeah, I remember. Well, Denny, the commute hour is long gone is why I get the slackers. You must have a shit-hot job to leave it till after the morning rush before headin' to work. More'n half the time you're my only pick-up this time o' day."

The younger man stabbed a finger at the drift.

"And I might be the last if you don't get behind the damn wheel."

Yodel just kept on grinning.

"Ah, no worries, Denny, Yodel'll get you there safe

Streaker

and sound. And with a warble or two from the old country into the bargain. Just you sit tight and relax."

As he sidled back along the side to his wheelhouse, Yodel gave a yodel.

Traeger shook his head. Went to sit just as Yodel opened the throttle. Pegasus jerked Traeger off balance. He slapped his left hand down on the seat alongside him to not topple after a hard tail landing. Shook his head again, lips munching, before putting his briefcase between his feet and opening his newspaper.

Pegasus swung to starboard to aim up the channel between the nearest rank of moored boats and the ends of stub jetties from the near shore. She chugged up to speed.

Homes on steep waterfront blocks slid by the port gunwale. Over the chug, yodelling.

Traeger read his paper.

Soon the foreshore fell away toward the open end of the bay. On the point, dense bush separated a large brown house from its neighbours. In front, a boathouse, jetty and pontoon with swim steps.

Traeger lifted his head to eye-graze the scenery. His eyes suddenly widened and stared as a woman emerged dripping from the sea onto the pontoon. She walked up the ramp onto the jetty. Picked up a towel.

She was in her thirties. Full-bodied. Shapely. Nude.

And apparently oblivious of her nudity, or that she might have attracted an observer.

Traeger closed his mouth but couldn't seem to bring his eyebrows down from their lift of disbelief. He tore his eyes from her for the moment it took to scan the bay for any other witness to the event.

No one, apparently. And no break in the yodelling suggested not even Yodel.

The fact that the sight was his and his alone made him uneasy. As if he were a voyeur. Which urged him to divert his attention elsewhere. An urge overcome by his curiosity about her next move.

He watched as she slung the towel over her left shoulder and began the walk along the jetty to the shore as if he wasn't there. As if the ferry wasn't there.

Her hip-swing was hypnotic. Traeger couldn't take his eyes off her retreating beauty. Suddenly had another thought.

"Oh, what a moron!"

He dived into his pocket. Fumbled so badly that he knocked his sunnies off. Dropped his paper recovering his glasses. Got his hands on his smartphone, but not before the breeze took the paper apart and blew most of it overboard. He cursed its loss. Aimed. Shot multiple frames.

The woman dropped off the land end of the jetty, passed behind the boathouse, reappeared on the zigzag path up the block's incline. Trees and the towel over her near shoulder tantalised. At each glimpse, he let go a volley of shots.

Looked up, frustrated by the intervening shrubbery denying him a clear shot.

"C'mon. C'mon. Without these ..."

One last glimpse — he taking what he could get — and she vanished out of sight virtually at the brown house, not once showing full face.

After a long stare after her, Traeger raised his phone to his eyes and shielded it with his free hand to see what he had. Not much.

"... who'd believe me? My shrink? No way. She just asks questions I can't answer. As it is, Schebel will probe and probe and ..."

Streaker

3: The shrink

Sternly gorgeous, Dr Laura Shebel frowned at her patient's phone. Her eyes went to the naked woman's right shoulder. To the tiny splodge, which, despite its size, Shebel saw as the tattoo of a seahorse.

Mid-forties, the psychologist was in a severe grey suit cut to show off her figure but that said "all business". Bunned brown hair and black-framed glasses. Sparse jewellery.

Her rooms almost as sparse. Desk under the drapeless window, chair backed to the view over Macquarie Street. Built-in library shelving over all of one wall, book spines aligned as properly as parading soldiers. A cabinet tailored to take a sound system, TV monitor, video recorder and camera on tripod. Two deep leather lounge chairs opposed over a long low coffee table, their rolled arms as broad as fat Labradors.

On the arm of her chair, a notepad. Also a voice recorder, which pointed at the armchair opposite her where Traeger sat poking one of the arms and studying the way the leather took its time recovering from dimple to smooth again.

In the background music played. Dully repetitive. Utterly unmelodious. A heavy beat as edgy as a

13

migraine throb despite its low volume.

"That was just the Monday. I got a virtual replay Tuesday and then again on Thursday. Repeats so identical I didn't bother with re-shoots. As it is, I'll have trouble explaining to Shanta if she ever gets to see my phone full of nudes. And that was just last week. Then it was on again this morning."

He took his phone back from manicured hands.

"So what was different about the off days?"

Her voice elided as slickly as blades on ice.

"Other late commuters or the odd housewife got on the ferry with me. Someone's got to be playing a joke."

"Why do you say that?"

"No one else sees this woman. She only appears when I'm the sole passenger and comes out of the water precisely at the time I'm passing her jetty."

"Otherwise the skipper ... this ..." She consulted her notepad. "Yodel, would see her. And you say he doesn't."

He shook his head.

"And not two minutes later, when we'd be past the headland and out of sight. It's too weird."

In the pause while Schebel made a note in her steno pad, he turned his head toward the sound system. Munched his lips.

"Do we have to have that damn noise?"

"Not if it bothers you."

She rose, went to the sound system, cut the music and took her place again.

"Why does it, Denny?

She studied her patient.

"It just puts my nerves on edge."

She studied the nervy way he unwrapped gum and chewed. She avoided penning a note then but would later. It was the third session in a row he had objected to *Through Silver in Blood* by Neurosis, which is why she

Streaker

had put it on just before he came this time. She would experiment with other thudding syncopation in future sessions to see if it was significant.

But right now it was time to broach the real issue.

"Is there anything about this repeated sighting that suggests a connection with your past?"

"You're determined to blame my problem at home on my memory hole. My dissociative amnesia, as you call it. And I keep telling you, a single missing day as a fifteen-year-old can't be anything to do with anything."

"Yet there must be some reason why your wife can't conceive. You must know that or you wouldn't keep coming to see me."

"I only keep coming because Shanta and her damn father insist on it."

"Surely you can understand your wife wanting children after ..." A glance again at her notes. "... almost four years. We have had it confirmed that there is no *physiological* reason why your sperm count is down. And you yourself have admitted to low libido."

"I'm not ready to have kids yet. I told you, while I'm tied up in this senate subcommittee work ..."

"As Senator Candy's press secretary. Yes, I remember. Important work, I agree, formulating new policy on refugee children in detention. But your persistent reluctance to discuss your past sexual relationships suggests your problem goes back well before Shanta."

He jogged his knees to stamp his heels audibly, and frowned.

"Then, I was tied up studying to make sure I got a scholarship to do media studies, what with a mum barely able to feed what was left of our family after my father ... well, you know."

"An admirable focus. But you also had to have a life beyond work."

Robin duMerrick

He looked to be about to argue. Instead, consulted his watch. Made to stand.

"Speaking of work ..."

"We still have a few minutes. Tell me, Denny, is it possible that your mind is doubling up on this swimmer episode as a way of goading you into letting go the past event we're trying to set free?"

"Doubling up? As in reruns that aren't really happening? I just showed you the phone pics, damn it."

"I'm not disputing the original episode. However, you said yourself that it's improbable that on ... what, four occasions? ... there has not been a single other witness."

He stood, hands clenched.

"Oh, so now this Streaker is my *in*fertile imagination working overtime, eh? Well it's nothing of the kind. I'll prove it."

"Denny ..."

But he was already on the march to the door. If it didn't actually slam behind his exit, it wasn't far short of it.

#

"So, what do you think?"

Schebel half-cocked her head at the voice behind her.

Cassandra Koh skirted Schebel's chair. Koh had a plain dark blue jacket finger-hooked over her shoulder. She cast the jacket over the back of the lounge. Flopped in the chair just vacated by Traeger. Leant back, revealing a police badge on her belt.

Koh's doll looks clearly came from an Asian heritage. Her tough stance and demeanour did not. Her figure was boy-like, small-breasted. In jeans, red sleeveless open-collared shirt. Short black hair tied in a stubby pony tail. On her left wrist, a mannish wide

16

Streaker

leather band with a chunky watch set into it. Around her neck, a leather strop choker hanging a silver bullet. On her feet, Brooks walkers.

Schebel's eyes drifted down Koh then up before speaking.

"You know I have reservations about this."

"I distinctly heard you tell him again that the reason he scores zip on the fatherhood index is a mind thing."

The voice rang with no Asian chimes. It was cold, matter-of-fact. Cop-speak.

"Fundamentally, yes. Psychological trauma *can* affect hormone control in the pituitary's production of sperm."

"The same trauma bad enough for him to bury in a memory hole so deep that two months of these bull sessions have done zip to dig up."

No sneer to it. Just the cadence of scepticism.

The shrink registered no offence.

"And it could take months more, even with the radical strategy we have embarked upon. Although I have my doubts it is going to help *you*."

"And yet you've conceded it's possible the murder I'm trying to solve could — if it figures in your patient's past in any way — be behind his blank spot."

"His being prompted to come to me with these mystery nude swimmer episodes has added nothing to our understanding of what your quest has to do with mine."

"Mm, we'll see. Just keep the faith."

Koh rose and turned to go. Schebel's eyes dropped momentarily to the tight derriere in the tight jeans.

"That rain-check is still open, Cassie. I'm done here by seven if you're free."

Koh grabbed up her coat, slung it over her shoulder. Headed for the door, opened it, turned back.

Her black eyes hadn't once blinked through the

dialogue. Didn't blink now fixed on Schebel.

"Working Cold Case doesn't allow much time for socialising. Remind me again when we know your patient is not my killer."

She left.

Schebel remained staring at the closing door.

Streaker

4: Spin

The bridge walkers crawled over the Sydney Harbour arch a hundred and thirty metres above the water and three floors lower than the carpet-to-ceiling windows of Senator Arthur Candy's office.

Glass partitioned off space for the senator's staff at their desks.

The office showed a love of things Japanese. A mural of intertwined dragons across the inner wall. A furoshiki hanging of Kanagawa's Great Wave on the wall opposite the eight-shelf bookcase. Tea service, chiyogami napkins and a pair of cherry blossom silk fans artfully arranged on a kotatsu table. A desk gong and bonsai on the black lacquered table serving as a desk by the window. Just inside the door, a valet hanging a black silk kimono alongside an expensive dark grey suit jacket.

Arthur Candy sat in shirtsleeves and vest at his desk, bent over 10x8 photos arrayed in three rows of four. He studied them through gold-rimmed peepers he only needed for reading.

He swapped two of the snaps, reappraised, swapped another two.

He was spare-framed. Handsome. Immaculate.

19

Robin duMerrick

Wavy hair expertly dyed to leave distinguished grey tips. Tummy tight from lunch-break workouts.

Not bad for a sixty-nine-year-old, his staff felt obliged to tell him often.

He beckoned at a door knock.

Denny Traeger entered, chewing gum. He held a sheet of paper. Headed for a guest chair.

Without looking up, Candy held his hand out.

"Ah, my response to that arsehole, McGirk."

He read.

"Good, good. It's easy for our critics to say we ought to have an open door policy on boat people. If the opposition ever get into power — heaven forbid — they'll soon change their tune."

Denny Traeger never argued full on with his boss.

"Still, Arthur, you have to admit the direction the subcommittee's heading leaves us open to criticism. Continuing your longstanding scheme of billeting the kids into the community is admirable enough. But doing so while keeping their mums and dads in detention pending vetting is going to cop some flack."

Candy plucked the nearest photograph off the desk and passed it to Traeger. It was of a ten year-old Tamil boy. He wore hand-me-downs. Was cute, but looked sad.

"Look at this sweet innocent face. How can we keep the likes of these locked up? It isn't their fault that their parents flouted immigration law to jump the queue and enter our country illegally."

Traeger returned the snap, which was placed carefully back in its spot among similar boy and girl shots.

"It's just that it seems to outsiders that you're driving the agenda when it's supposed to be an exercise in presenting *all* the options for policy change."

"I can't worry about appearances. Besides, we

Streaker

have the public behind us. They want a tough policy on immigration but don't like the idea of children in custody any more than the bleeding hearts. The recommendation we're heading for will ease many a conscience and frankly, Denny, is the right thing to do."

"Hey, you don't have to convince me, Arthur. Who knows what abuse those kids are suffering in detention? Then there was that rash of kids on a release program who went mysteriously missing, never to be seen again. Makes me sick to think about it."

"Quite. Forgive me asking, but have you got problems at home? You seem uncharacteristically distracted."

"The same old same old. Shanta's father is grizzling about her not starting a family. Blames me."

Candy's eyebrows flickered up in slight curiosity.

"And you're not ready for children?

"When we wrap up this subcommittee work, maybe." Paused a beat. "So that'll also do as a hand-out at the press conference?

"Nicely. And it wouldn't hurt if you had a blow-up done for behind me at the lectern."

Candy passed the photograph of the Tamil boy to Traeger.

"This one ought to wring a tear from the lady reporters at the very least. Call me five minutes after the hounds are all seated with pens and recorders poised."

5: Home life

Denny Traeger leapt ashore off the deck of an idling Pegasus at the ferry wharf. He was one of seven commuters bound for home after their day at work.

Traeger carried his briefcase, his jacket draped over it. He passed Yodel holding the vessel in against the wharf.

Long shadows blackened the water lapping the eastern side of the jetty.

"See ya in the morning, Danny."

"Denny." Teeth slightly gritted.

"Oh, yeah." Not the least put out. "See ya in the morning, Denny. I'll save you a yodel."

Traeger walked off the jetty. Turned left onto the path that ran along the front of the steep waterfront gardens. Paused at his old paddleboard on the sea wall. Started up the zig-zag path to the house above. His house.

\#

Traeger paused at the back door opening onto the steep garden gradient. He reached for the handle only to have it swing inward before he could work it.

His wife, Shanta, surprised him standing there. Her face was stern, its perfect skin stretched in stress.

Streaker

They didn't kiss. He pushed past.

She stood forlorn, her willowy Indian body stiff, wrapped in a sari, sandalled feet unmoving, waiting for her husband to lead a conversation she knew would end as it always did.

He dropped his briefcase and jacket.

"Don't tell me. Your father's here. You only ever go traditional when he's about to show up."

She closed the door.

"It pleases him."

He moved along the corridor. She followed.

"You know I don't like it. The way it flattens your boobs. You look more like a small boy than a grown woman. It makes me squirm."

He shuddered. She sighed, seeing it.

"I'll change when he goes. I'm sorry, I tried to call you."

"What is it, more of the same? I'm sick and tired of his harping on it."

"You make it sound like he is being unreasonable."

"We don't always get everything we want when we want it." He turned to study her face. "Did you tell him?"

"About the tests? Yes."

"Then that's his answer, damn it. Let's get this over with."

He opened the door into the living room. Stepped into the light flooding through the picture window giving a view of Elvina Bay.

The room was a statement of his-and-hers disharmony.

Hers: Tapestries on the wall. Temple scenes in embossed teak panels the colour and shine of hazelnut shells. Carved dark-wood furniture. A china cabinet crammed with elephants in ebony, and incense censures and ashtrays the shape of a lady's slender hand.

Robin duMerrick

His: Leather-fronted bar. Trophies on a modern sound-system sideboard. In front, a framed photo of a grinning young Traeger in a fishing kayak, a rod in one hand, a giant Spanish mackerel over his lap. Framed on the wall, a Walkley Award, his name on it. And a complete DVD set of Andrea Bocelli.

Manu Chand stood looking out the window, hands clasped behind him. A small man, dressed smart casual, expensively. His voice a chime despite the damping of bouncing it off the glass back to those approaching behind him.

"A charming view. Not only of a magnificent bay, but affording a peek into the waterside gardens of the privileged. I would wager you see all manner of odd goings-on around these waterfronts from time to time."

Traeger frowned at having to speak to his father-in-law's back. Also spared a frown for the Gucci attache case on the coffee table, which the old fox only toted around when he was selling someone on something.

"What sort of odds things would you expect we see?"

Shanta hovered at the door, unsure. Her father turned. Propped on the near settee's backrest facing them.

He smiled his permanent smile showing too-perfect white teeth. Black hair coiffed from a central part. He wore cream sports slacks, black shirt, cream silk cravat, a gold signet ring.

"You tell *me*, my boy. I get to see the wealthy at play often enough. Amusing, but still only from their polished facade side of things. Wouldn't I like to peek into their back door lives like you, once in a while? How are you, anyway, Denny?"

Chand skirted the settee. Put an arm around Traeger's shoulders and steered him to the settee.

"I was looking forward to unwinding in a quiet

Streaker

evening at home, to tell you the truth."

Chand chose not to hear the edge in his son-in-law's retort.

"And so you shall. As soon as we've had our little talk."

The Indian turned to his daughter.

"Would you mind leaving us to a brief man-chat, Shanta dear?"

Not a question. A command.

Shanta Traeger left without a word. Chand took the settee opposite Traeger's. Lounged back, in charge.

"I'm not going to insult your intelligence, Denny my boy. You know my agenda as well as I do. I'm not going to live forever, and before I go, I want the pleasure of having grandchildren around me."

He waited for a reaction. Didn't get one.

"It isn't all selfishness at work, either. Shanta, too, is long overdue the fruits of motherhood. Heavens above man, you two have been married now for going on four years. What's the problem? Doesn't she do it for you any longer? You can be frank here. I have a solution for that. In fact I have a solution for everything. Out with it."

"You know about the tests. Shanta told me she spilt the beans."

Chand waved it aside.

"Tosh. As long as you're not actually shooting blanks, a fertile young woman like Shanta will conceive. What do the doctors know anyway? Unless you can't get it up. I've got a solution for that as well."

"Just because you can sell steel by the mega-ton to third world government cronies doesn't make you a marriage counsellor." Rasped low. But making no impression.

"I didn't get rich taking 'no' for an answer, either. If Shanta isn't doing it for you, I can arrange for whoever does. A more *professional* woman, shall we say, who can

25

work you into a frenzy enough to want to finish the job where it needs to be finished."

"A whore?" Incredulous.

"Not at all. I know a sex therapist who will go to any lengths. It's done all the time."

Chand leant forward. Unsnapped the attache case. Thrust a 6x4 photo at Traeger.

"Bonny is stunning, yes? You see her there at a window in the apartment she has taken short-term across the way from her ... er, client ... with instructions for him to signal when his partner goes to bed, then to watch. Bonny strips like so, holding him in a voyeur's grip of Bonny's, shall we say, 'solo performance'. He is aroused. He takes it to his wife's bed and *bingo*."

Traeger's eyes went wide.

"You didn't ...!"

"Didn't what?" Puzzled.

"Hire Bonny to do a skinny-dipping solo number on me."

"What? No. Why, does that appeal? If so ..."

"No. Look, this is getting silly. I'm done with this. You go or stay, suit yourself. As for me, I'm going paddling."

Traeger stomped to the door. Wrenched it open. Shanta stood there, anxiously waiting to be summoned.

"I'm through with your father. Any time he's here, I'm not. Make certain of it."

Traeger paced down the corridor. Ripped off shirt, pants, shoes, socks, barely breaking stride. Grabbed a two-bladed paddle from the corner by the door. Stormed out. Slammed the door behind him.

Streaker

6:Fallon Hall

Traeger's pecs flexed in an easy rhythm. The paddleboard surged with each dip and rake of strong arms. Each stroke took him further from his home and further from his state of agitation.

The waterfronts slid by. He came abreast of the steps where he had seen the Streaker from the deck of Pegasus.

A dinghy was wedged under the Streaker's jetty at its bow by a rising tide, its motor canted into the air, its bow about to go under.

He paddled in, leapt onto the pontoon and dragged his board on. He glanced up at the brown house, half expecting someone to yell at his trespass. No one did.

The house was on two levels. The upper level had a full-width balcony in front. The lower level opened onto a patio reached through double doors at the top of the winding garden path.

He shrugged and freed the dinghy. It drifted until brought up at the end of its painter. He looked up again, debating. Suddenly made up his mind. Muttered his decision to himself.

"Why not clear this up once and for all?"

He marched along and off the jetty and started up

Robin duMerrick

the steep zig-zag garden path to the house.

At the open double doors, he knocked, his eyes lingering over the polished brass plaque with *FALLON HALL* engraved on it. It looked new.

He peered inside past the double doors, sure someone would come. Sure she would be fully clothed, not sure he would recognise her either way.

His eyes adjusted to the low light enough to see it was a rumpus room. Bar in the left corner. A stairway to upstairs from where music played. He recognised the *Pirates of the Caribbean*'s *Yo Ho, Yo Ho*.

Suddenly, over it, a voice. A man's.

"Hello, hello. Be right there."

Legs appeared on the stairway, followed by a big soft bulk of a man in his sixties, with a cheery face, cheeks florid. Wearing torn khaki cargo shorts and a striped French sailor shirt. Buckle-up sandals.

"I'm sorry to intrude but ..."

"Nonsense, nonsense. Welcome aboard. I saw what you did. Come in, come in." Then loudly. "Clara. Bring some beers down, will you, hon? It's the kind fellow who saved the tinny from a drowning. And turn that music down, will you?"

The music faded. The big man pulled Traeger toward the bar, which was topped with a small fake keg and some nautical knickknacks. Traeger let himself be ushered to a bar stool. He perched, but his attention was on the stairs.

"It's okay. I'm not much of a beer person anyway. And I can't drink and paddle."

"Like not drinking and driving, eh? You live in the bay, I can tell. You know boats. I can always tell a man who knows boats. I was in the Navy you know. I'm John Wentworth, by the way."

He held his hand out to shake Traeger's. Raised his voice again. "Those beers, hon. Come and say hello."

28

Streaker

Then with a wink, his voice confidential: "Clara's hearing's not what it was. Played viola for years in symphony orchestras all over the world. All that drum banging and cymbal clanging takes its toll, you know."

Traeger sat bolt upright at the footfall on the stairs, craning for an early look at, surely, his Streaker.

A silken contralto preceded the new arrival.

"Hold your horses. I told you to stock the bar, didn't I, John."

She floated down the stairs, a theatrical entrance despite carrying a six-pack. A small woman of sixty or so in a floral dress and white sandals with a flower at the toe. A little plump but still a good figure. Hair dyed reddish, but tending more toward strawberry blond. A flower pinned to one side.

Traeger studied her as she put the beers on the bar. John Wentworth reached for a can impatiently and snapped it. She turned to Traeger. Extended a hand as if he should kiss it.

"What handsome young man has come to visit? And you are ...?"

Traeger studied her. Could she be his Streaker?

"Denny Traeger. I live up the end of the bay from you."

John Wentworth offered beers, was ignored. Slurped his own.

"What is it, Denny? You're looking at me as if I might be your long lost nanny." Her contralto full of mirth chimes.

He snapped out of it. But he couldn't help blurting out his confusion.

"I'm sorry if I was staring. Look, this sounds an odd thing to ask someone you've just met, but is it you I see skin ... er, taking a dip in the mornings? Ten-ish?"

"Oh good Lord no. You must have the wrong jetty. My skinny-dipping days are over ... Unless it was to

29

Robin duMerrick

scare the fish to death." She giggled. "You *were* going to say 'skinny-dipping'."

"Rubbish, m'dear. You're as smashing in the altogether as ever you were."

She curtsied.

"Nice of you to say, kind sir. But ..." She threw a mischievous grin at Traeger. "... we are embarrassing our guest."

"Not at all. But may I ask, are you two on your own? I mean, do you have children still living at home?"

The husband answered.

"All flown the coop. None too soon, either. They'd sponge off the old folks into their dotage if we let 'em."

She patted her husband's hand.

"He means do we have a daughter who skinny-dips off our jetty of a morning." Then to Traeger: "No, there's just us. But I'm intrigued. Are you sure it's *our* jetty?"

"Unless I'm as batty as some think I am."

Wentworth raised wiry eyebrows at his wife.

"Could be that Fallon woman."

"Oh?"

Clara Wentworth rose to it.

"The people we bought this place off. A bit over a year ago now. A brother and sister. She married and went to live overseas. The brother said he couldn't afford to keep Fallon Hall."

"But she's been back?"

"A flying visit to her brother from wherever she was. Do you remember, John?"

"Dubai, I think she said. Husband's an architect."

"Yes, I do believe it was. And she took the time to visit here. She asked if we minded her spending an hour fishing off the pontoon like she did as a youngster."

"To relive old memories, as it were."

"Of course we had no objection. Delightful young woman. Thanked us profusely before she left."

Streaker

"And you think she might've come back a second time?"

"Entirely possible."

"But we would have seen her, dear. Surely."

"Not if she walked around the waterfront track."

"Well, I suppose so." Doubt meted out the words slowly. But then she turned cheery, struck by a thought. "Then why not simply ask her brother, if it's such a source of curiosity? You've got his card here somewhere for forwarding his mail, John, remember?"

"By George, I think you're right, Clara. A woodworker, wasn't he?" He scrubbed his chin. "Now where did I ...? Ah, here somewhere, I think."

Wentworth vanished below the level of the bar. Bottles clinked and paper things rustled.

Clara rolled her eyes to Traeger.

"Really, he'd lose his ears if they weren't pinned to his noggin."

Wentworth appeared, jubilant. Slapped a card onto the bar.

"There, didn't I tell you?"

Traeger took the card. Stared at it.

#

The buzz saw sang from beyond the door. Traeger waited for the zing of the cut-off and the dying whine before knocking on the shed in the backyard of the house whose address was on the card the Wentworths had given him.

The man who opened the ill-fitting door with his foot was in his mid twenties. Built like a barrel. He had heavy features. Wore bib-front tan overalls and work boots.

His hands were busy sanding the cut-off end of a newly-turned chair leg.

"You're the fella that called. Danny ...?"

"Denny with an 'e'. Denny Traeger. Thanks for

31

Robin duMerrick

agreeing to see me."

The big man nodded. He didn't offer to shake hands. Instead, stepped aside, still holding the door open against its spring with a boot.

Traeger went in. Heard the door clunk behind him. Looked around at the clutter. Wood lathe, drill press, planer, tools on a shadowboard. A bandsaw slowing to a steely whisper. A broken chair in the bench's vice with one leg broken out. Sawdust and shavings everywhere.

"You said the Wentworths found an old card of mine. How *are* the sly old foxes?"

"Foxes? Sly? I found them delightful."

"Yeah. You weren't hard up, selling 'em a house. They're tougher than nails. Squeezed me drier than a prune in an olive press."

He spun the piece of sandpaper in his hand into a bin at the end of the bench and picked up a fresh square. Went on sanding the leg.

"Anyhow you didn't come to discuss the oldies. You want to know is my sister visiting. You think you might've seen her, what was it ...? Swimming off the old pontoon?"

"She'd fished off it before, the Wentworths were saying."

"Surprises me not. She loved the old place. Hated that we had to sell it. Frankly it didn't bother me none. Mum left it to both of us, but in the end, it was tidier for us to sell it and split the proceeds."

"So your sister *is* back home for a visit?"

"If she is, she hasn't told me. What's it to you, anyway?"

Traeger was ready with a lie.

"Whoever the swimmer was, she dropped some money. A few hundred. I saw it, passing on the ferry, but couldn't get back until later. Lucky it was still there. I asked the Wentworths who the swimmer was. They

32

Streaker

said it might be your sister."

"I'll get it to her if you like." Too eagerly. "If she's here, she'll call eventually."

"No, I'd best do it or hand it in to the police."

"Don't trust me, eh? Don't blame yer. I wouldn't trust me neither with that much money." Took a deep breath. "Okay, so what did this dame look like?"

"I'm not very good at describing people. You wouldn't have a photograph of her by any chance?"

"Well ... Not so's it'll do you much good."

Fallon put down the chair leg and sandpaper. Took his wallet from his hip pocket. Opened it and slipped out a dog-eared colour photo. Passed it to Traeger.

"Family wasn't big on snaps. This is it, pretty much. Bit long in the tooth."

Traeger stared at the snap of a woman in her late twenties holding two kids on a paddleboard afloat. The boy about eight, the girl a year or two younger, were in bathing suits. Little more than the back of the woman's head and her bare shoulder were in shot.

The mother wore a light tan halter-neck top. She had untidy red hair. On the bared right shoulder was the tattoo of a seahorse.

"Taken at Whale Beach. Helluva hot it was that day." He went on sanding. "As I said, not much good to you."

But Traeger was not listening. He reached for his phone. Wrenched it out of his pocket. Thumbed it. Peered at it. Thumbed it again.

The screen of the phone displayed one of the stills he took of the Streaker and showed his shrink. He zoomed the phone. On the Streaker's right shoulder, the tattoo of a seahorse.

He compared snap and phone images. He gushed, startling the stockier man.

"*That's her*. I recognise the tattoo on her shoulder.

That's who I saw on the Wentworth's jetty, no doubt about it."

"Huh? You're scaring me now, man."

"Scaring you? What do you mean?"

"I mean you ain't no clairvoyant, right? Sis ain't got no tattoo on her shoulder or anywhere else. She's that kid with me when I was eight. You're looking at our mum. And it can't be her you saw. She's been dead seventeen years."

Streaker

7: Ghost

Laura Schebel sat alone at a table. Dressed for the office, eating a salad, her attention on the water view, oblivious to the buzz of other diners around her.

She was sipping her one allowed glass of white when a voice nearby caused her to spill a little wine.

"Laura ... Oh! Sorry, Doc, I didn't mean to startle you. Your office said you were here."

Denny Traeger was clearly agitated. Carried a black document slipcase.

"Denny. I thought I was clear ..."

"No contact outside our sessions. Yes, I know. Except in emergencies, you said."

"Well, is this an emergency?"

Schebel's eyes dropped to the slipcase as if for clues.

"It most certainly is. Either I'm going mad or the rest of the world is. May I?"

She sighed, pushed the salad away.

"I wasn't enjoying this anyway. Well, don't just stand there, Denny. Sit. But let me warn you, if your problem can't be resolved in the time it takes for me to finish my wine, then you'll have to make an appointment or wait until our next session on Thursday."

Robin duMerrick

He hastened to seat himself. Blurted it out.

"Laura, I've just seen a ghost. At least that's what they'd have me believe."

"Who's they?"

"I've just come from the son of the Streaker. A Leith Fallon."

"How on earth did you manage to track her son down?"

"That doesn't matter. What does is that he gave me an old photograph."

He dug a magnifier from his slipcase. Then a dog-eared photograph paper-clipped to a sheet of paper. He placed the paperwork in front of her. Slipped off the paper-clip and put the photograph and paper side-by-side. Waved a hand across the pair, inviting a comparison.

"On the way here, I stopped by the office and printed off a blow-up of one of the shots I took on my phone. You know, of the very first swim."

He unwrapped gum and chewed as he studied her studying his offerings.

Schebel really didn't need the glance she took to know about the similarity between the subject of the printout and that of the photograph.

She met his eyes.

"So it seems you've identified the swimmer. Is that a problem for you?"

"It does when she's been dead for seventeen years."

He pushed the magnifier forward across the table.

"Dead?"

"Drowned. Found floating In Pittwater without a stitch on. Maybe foul play, maybe not."

"You think they're one and the same because both have red hair?" She put a sceptical lilt to it.

"Look again. The sea horse tattoos. Identical."

He poked the magnifier closer to her. She took it up

Streaker

and made a show of eyeballing his printout, then the photo.

He pressed.

"It *has* to be the same woman."

"Then ... Perhaps the son is wrong about his mother drowning. She may have simply walked away from her life and family. People do it all the time."

"*He and his sister inherited the family home, for Christ's sake*."

The eyes of diners at adjacent tables homed in on the source of the outburst. He muted his postscript.

"You can't do that with the doubtful dead."

"Then it must be two different women. Seahorse tattoos cannot be that uncommon. It is the only answer. What did the brother say?"

"That I was nuts if I thought I'd seen his mother just a few days ago. If that were so, he said, then the cops were wasting their time reopening the case."

"Reopening the investigation into his mother's death?"

"A detective from Cold Case had been to see him only last week, he said. A ..." He took a card from his slipcase. "... Detective Sergeant Cassandra Koh."

Schebel's expression didn't alter.

"Who would undoubtedly give you the same likely explanations you've heard from me." Then an afterthought. Or was it? "Of course, there is another explanation, which I think we need to explore in our next session."

"What's that?"

"You did say this drowning happened seventeen years ago? And, moreover, in your playground: Pittwater."

"That's what Leith Fallon said."

"Did you think to take seventeen years off your age and come up with the year you were fifteen? The

37

Robin duMerrick

year you suffered that memory blank while a teen in Pittwater?"

"What of it?"

"We know that the trigger for your dissociative amnesia was some traumatic event at the time. Could it be that your preoccupation with your swimmer is your mind trying to tell you that the trauma has something to do with the death of Fallon's mother?"

He snorted.

"I don't believe that for a second. As I keep telling you, my getting drunk and waking up with no memory of the day before is all there is to it."

"Nonetheless, I want you to think about it between now and our Thursday session. Ask yourself could your subconscious be using your swimmer sightings in an effort to prise open the painful memory of a completely different swimmer. The one who drowned seventeen years ago?"

"Nonsense. Something like that I'd remember. I know I would."

"Perhaps. However, you might change your mind if you were to learn that the drowning and your memory blank occurred on the same day."

Her pause was deliberate, giving him a moment to consider before dangling the bait.

"I think you would be advised to ask this Cold Case detective ... this Sergeant Koh ... what the police know about this drowning. It might pay off for you both."

He swallowed the hook. Snatched up the images and magnifier. Stuffed them back in the slipcase and stood.

"Okay, I will. Just to prove you wrong."

He marched out through the tables without a glance back at his doctor.

#

Denny Traeger stood naked in front of the bathroom mirror.

Streaker

The bath's cold water was running. The bathroom door locked, even with Shanta out shopping. Alongside the bath on the floor, two ornamental buckets from the bar big enough to bed a magnum of champagne in ice cubes. Now, they held no bottles, just the ice. To the brim.

Taped to the mirror were three photographs, and a fourth image on paper, printed after uploading it from his phone to his computer. The Streaker. Top left corner of the mirror.

Three of the images were of nudes. The one to the right of the printout was the 6x4 his stepfather had left behind after their "man-chat". Of Bonny, the sex-therapist said to turn on laggardly libidos by putting on a self-pleasuring show for her clients, as she was in the photo now before him.

The one next right, of his wife in a pose that was intended to be provocative but was demure compared with Bonny's. Shanta had had it shot professionally in a desperate attempt to ignite passion enough in her husband to get pregnant. The smile on her face was strained. Every muscle in her body tense. Like a self-conscious schoolgirl taking a naked selfie to text to her boyfriend, believing that's what today's girlfriends do.

Traeger's mind browsed such impressions as his eye passed over this trio.

But it was the third photo, under the others by itself, that commanded most of his attention.

It was of a mid-teen. A little lingering puppy-fat close to dissolving into pleasing curves. Short black hair. Cute round button-nosed face. In the short black skirt and low-cut white blouse that was the kitchen and bar girls' uniform in his father's pub.

Her name was Charlene. He had been fifteen. She had come to his room one Saturday in summer before her shift when his parents were flat out in the bar. They

39

had made fumbling love. For him, his first time and, he believed, hers as well. It had happened again three times. His eyes were so filled with the image of her body after sex that he had wanted to retain it in a photo shot on his phone. But she had not let him. So he'd had to make do with a photograph of her after she'd dressed. The photo he stared at now.

A week after that, she didn't turn up for work, never to be seen at the pub again. Or heard from. Not a word of explanation. It had hurt him deeply. But not as much as when he'd found out why.

The memory prompted him to check out his reflection. His lips curled into a snarl at his erection. The memory of the "why" should have killed it. Instead it only confirmed that he had no control over the evil that dwelt within him. The evil that he had inherited from his father.

He let the erection grow. Encouraged it by letting his imagination run riot, despite his disgust with it, over the images of the naked women. But mostly — which brought the most pain — of Charlene.

He waited for the urge he knew would come to clutch his erection and masturbate. The urge he knew most men would succumb to. Even embrace. Without a trace of the guilt surging within him now.

He waited until it was virtually overwhelming. Then, with a scowl at his reflection, he spun, turned off the bath tap, dumped both buckets of ice into the bath, climbed into it and forced himself fully immersed in the freezing water.

He gritted his teeth against the impulse to relieve the pain.

But at least his erection would not survive.

Streaker

8: Cold case cop

Detectives took most of the second floor of the LAC — the Local Area Command — that dealt with the northern peninsula suburbs including Pittwater. A landscaped office, with two desks abreast in three rows, some desks occupied. Opposite the entrance, on the side with the best views, an expanse of glass partitioned off the chief's office. By the entrance, a desk, occupied by a civilian clerk.

Detective Sergeant Cassandra Koh had a visitor sitting in a borrowed chair at the end of her desk. In her estimation, a visitor good looking but worry-faced in a way she had seen on many a guilty man.

She made a show of studying the dog-eared photo through his magnifier before putting it down alongside his printout. Pierced him with her skewer-black eyes.

"So what scam are you pulling, Tiger?"

"Traeger. I told you my name is Traeger. Denny Traeger."

She shrugged.

"Traeger, Tiger. All you *gwai-lo* names sound the same to Chink ears."

"You're being funny, right?"

"I don't have time to be funny. So what is it? You

Robin duMerrick

got your girlfriend to use a rub-on tat the same as in the old snap from the Fallon kids. Got her to take a stroll in the raw. Shot it and brought it along to me so I'd think Felicity Fallon was still alive?"

"Felicity? Was that her name?"

"As if you didn't know. What I want to know, Tiger, is what's your angle?"

His sigh suggested he'd given up over the abuse of his name.

"Look I'm as puzzled by this as you are. I can only tell you what I saw. You make what you want of it. All I ask is that you tell me what you can about this Fallon woman's death."

"If you're not here to jerk a cop around, what's it to you?"

This time his sigh was for having to admit bitter truths, presumably in a bid to earn some credibility with a hard-nosed cop.

"My therapist thinks it might have some bearing on a day missing from my memory of seventeen years ago when I was fifteen, living in Pittwater."

"*Bingo* on the year. Same as Fallon was fatally dunked. But what date was it your memory went AWOL?"

"Some time in early February. Teenagers don't do dates."

Koh opened a casefile on her desk.

"If it turns out to be February 6 that year, you've got my attention, Tiger."

"Is that when Felicity Fallon drowned?"

"Found on the seventh. Drowned the night before. Does your shrink think your conscience is hiding how you killed someone maybe?"

"Hell, no! Not for one moment."

His immediate frown could've been a moment's reflection.

42

Streaker

"If she does, she's wrong. I'm no killer. She did suggest it was something I maybe saw. But I know I'd remember anything vaguely like that."

"That's the point, Tiger. If you're to be believed, you *don't* remember. And badly enough that your shrink thinks she needs to treat you for ... What is it that she's treating you for, anyway? Not just you keep misplacing your car keys."

Embarrassment touched his good looks. Which accounted for his hesitation.

"She thinks it could be causing ... a loss of ... sexual function."

"Can't get it up, eh?" She feigned regret at the dejection her bluntness caused. "Hey, no big deal. Half the guys I know have the same problem."

But contrition, for her, was at best a two-second deal. She beckoned at him with wriggled fingers.

"So, gimme."

"Pardon."

It brought him back from the brink of self-pity.

"The full story. Gimme."

He seemed to regain some composure. Cocked his chin at her in defiance.

"I will if you will. All about Felicity Fallon. I need to know."

She stared a second. Suddenly tilted back in her chair and waved the printout and photo at the civilian clerk at the entrance to *Detectives*.

The clerk didn't seem to notice.

"I'll tell you what ..."

She interrupted herself, raising her voice as she waved the note.

"*Lowie. Got a job for you.*"

The clerk raised his billiard ball of a head. Trotted forward, took the paperwork with a knowing grin.

"Copies, right? For the casefile. Originals back to the

43

client."

"Make it quick."

The clerk trotted to the copy machine by his desk. The machine flashed light slices twice to a slither sound.

Koh stood. Swept her blue jacket off the back of her chair and grabbed the casefile off the desk.

"My need to solve a seventeen year old murder trumps your sexual black hole, Tiger. But I'll cut you a deal."

He looked up, puzzled. She beckoned, half turned away. Got one arm into a coat sleeve as she headed for the door.

As she went, she exchanged looks with "Lowie". His barely perceptible nod acknowledging that Operation Lookalike was now under way. And she had virtually not drawn a breath in her speech over her shoulder at the man still shuffling to this feet by her desk.

"I'll give you the grand tour, Tiger, if, on the way, you fill me in what you remember before and after your black hole."

The clerk held the originals out for Traeger to grab as he hurried by to catch up with the cop on her way out.

Streaker

9: Catch a cab

A late model Holden Commodore hummed by on a long curve heading east on the waterfront road fringing the southern shore of Pittwater. The sun was hot, its rays squint-sharp off the sea.

The driver was Detective Sergeant Cassandra Koh. Alongside her, Denny Traeger. Koh had just put down her mobile phone. She had not had it on hands-free.

"That call-back was from the office. Both Water Police launches are out on calls. Lowie's booked the water taxi for eleven for us."

"We'll be a few minutes late."

"They'll wait."

"Not if a fare comes along first."

"I'll bet you a roll in the hay."

"That confident, huh?"

"Assuming I care if I lose."

"Am I being hit on by a cop?"

"Not on duty, you're not. Now shelve the bullshit and get on with your story."

They were passing the marina on the last stub promontory before Church Point. She spared him a glance after his first few words of personal history.

"So you were a pub orphan."

45

"I guess so. The only time I ever saw either of my folks was behind a bar. I got myself off to school even before they were awake in the mornings. They drank with the patrons. I can't remember a night they didn't lock up the premises smashed."

"So you became a child of Pittwater instead."

"You could say that. I had an old kayak rigged with rod-holders and all the gear I could beg, borrow or steal. I'd chuck it in the water and go fishing every chance I got. Just to get away from that stinking pub."

"So I guess there wouldn't be much of Pittwater you don't know better than the angle of your dangle."

"You do have a way with words for a ..."

"For a Chink?"

"I was going to say a cop."

"That's okay. I'm permitted introverted racism. The point is, it's odd you living in Palm Beach and being Pittwater-wise didn't include knowing the only lady driving water taxis."

"Fallon? Is that what she was?" And at her nod. "Since when does a fifteen year old catch taxis, water or otherwise?"

She didn't rise to it as she slowed past the long car park and pulled into a vacant slot outside the Pasadena Hotel at Church point. Switched off.

They got out. Walked together toward the ferry wharf pointing west across McCarrs Creek to the forested slopes of Kuring-Gai Chase National Park.

She resumed her probing as they walked.

"Okay, so let's cut to the chase. What you do remember about what you don't remember?"

"I remember waking up with a massive hangover. Funny thing is, I never drank. I'm not much of a drinker now, but at fifteen, I couldn't stand the stink of it, the way it crept through the floorboards, even into the worm-hole we lived in over the bar."

Streaker

"So is that what your shrink is saying blotted out that day? A teen drinking binge?"

"No. I think she thinks it's to do with Mum announcing my father wasn't away at a convention as she'd told me for two weeks, but had gone to prison. For raping Charlene."

She propped for a moment to inspect his face.

"Holy shit. Who was Charlene?"

"A bar-girl not much older than me. She was the only one in the whole stinking place who had any time for me."

"So your Mum dropped that clanger *before* the drinking binge?"

"Actually I can't remember when she told me. The morning I woke with a hangover, I think."

She started walking. Took their first steps onto the scrubby grey timbers of the jetty.

"So let me get this straight. This shrink of yours. This ... what's her name again?"

"Laura Schebel."

"Right. Schebel. Is she saying it was the drinking binge blotted the bad shit, or the drinking binge *was* the bad shit, or learning your dear old dad was in the poky? Or that he'd stiffed Charlene? Or there was some other bad shit? Or all of the above. I'm confused."

"Huh. You're confused. Why do you reckon I'm seeing a shrink?"

They arrived at the boarding steps of the jetty just as the pink boat with a canopy and "Taxi" on his topsides idled in.

They let chat lapse as they watched the vessel bump alongside. Were further diverted by the head that jutted up at them from the side of the vessel.

If either of them found the fact that the driver was a woman, it wasn't worthy of comment. Not even that the woman was a redhead.

Robin duMerrick

The driver spoke, eyeing Traeger.

"A booking for a Mr Koh."

It was the detective who answered.

"That's a Msss. For Mackerel Beach."

The two passengers climbed aboard and sat together on one of the two seats running fore-and-aft on either side of the cockpit. Portside.

The driver steered away on idle. Her passengers didn't spare her a glance. If they had, and the helm seat hadn't hidden her back, they would've seen that she wore skimpy frayed-hem denim shorts and a tan, almost backless halter-neck top. Bare legs. Thongs.

Koh half-turned to Traeger sitting on her right.

"So the bad shit could be Felicity Fallon's drowning, which you say you didn't do."

"Which I most certainly didn't do."

"Or that you witnessed it, say."

"It occurred to me."

She jumped on that. Flashed an expectant look at him, hoping it was a breakthrough moment.

"So you think there might be something to it?"

"Not for a moment."

She grunted her minor deflation.

"Well, let's see if our little tour of the crime scene jostles the marbles."

#

The heavily wooded western shore of Pittwater slid by. His voice was raised slightly above the purr of the water taxi on cruise.

"You promised if I bared all, you would."

"Eh? Oh, yeah. Story-swap-wise, huh?"

She pulled the casefile from her bag at her feet, opened it and consulted the historical record.

"February 7 that year was a Tuesday. A commercial fisherman based in Patonga was laying his cray pots around 5 AM. He wondered why Pittwater's pink water

Streaker

taxi was adrift off Lion Island, apparently with no one aboard. He came into Palm Beach where he could get phone coverage and called the Water Police base up McCarrs Creek."

She extracted an old photo and put it in front of Traeger. He peered at it and wrinkled his nose.

"Jesus."

"Yeah, not a pretty sight with the sea's night feeders having had a go. That's how the Wateries pulled her from the drink."

He didn't need to interrupt over the slang for Water Police everyone used, even the Wateries themselves.

"Friends interviewed branded her a free spirit. No one was surprised that she might strip off for a swim starkers between fares."

Now he did need to interrupt.

"Out the open sea end of Pittwater? I don't think so. What time, do they know?"

"The medical examiner put the time of death at around nine the previous evening."

"Even more bizarre. I've swum every cove and bay in Pittwater, but the Barrenjoey Heads by the open sea at night where White Pointers have been known to hang out? No thanks."

"Well, it could be it wasn't her starting point. The boat and body both could've drifted out of ..." She swept her hand at the shallow bay of Portuguese Beach passing on their port side. "... one of these more secluded bays. Certainly when detectives searched the taxi, they found her clothes neatly folded, confirming the impromptu swim theory."

She drew breath.

"Which included the notion that a gust of wind had driven the boat out of reach for her to swim back and she drowned. The only thing was, the weather bureau said it had been an unusually still night. Hardly a breath of wind."

She didn't pause at the lift of his questioning eyebrow.

"For another, she wasn't known for being especially tidy. If she'd wanted to strip off for a splash, she wouldn't fold her clothes like they found them. But get this."

"I sense a slam dunk coming."

"She could apparently swim like a fish. She was a regular in the annual jetty-to-jetty marathons."

"Which are more than twice across Pittwater up that end."

"Right on. As for a slam dunk, no, it wasn't enough in the end for the coroner, who delivered an open finding."

The taxi slowed as it rounded the point into Mackerel Beach, allowing them to speak at usual volume.

"Is that all the cops of the day had?"

"They tried to find who'd used the water taxi service the previous night, but the logs were hopeless. This casefile ..." She tapped the file. "... also lists owners of holiday cottages in Pittwater's northern bays the cops interviewed to determine who was using them or letting them that night. Only one, a family spending a week in Mackerel, yielded anything."

They idled into the jetty at Mackerel. The taxi nudged the shadow-side of the jetty. The driver bolted from her swivel chair, stepped on the port seat and up onto the jetty. Grabbed a line.

Traeger stood. He took a step toward the opposite gunwale but suddenly propped, eyes on the driver's back as she made fast. He now saw more of her. A lot more.

The driver didn't seem to notice his apparent confusion.

"So you want me to wait, right?"

Streaker

Koh's response defied debate.

"For as long as it takes, honey."

"It'll cost you."

"Do I care?"

"In that case, take your time. Meanwhile ..."

The driver turned one-eighty to face into the sun, legs a-straddle. Threw her arms wide and her head back as if embracing the warmth, displaying lots of flesh.

"... I'll just stay here and soak up some rays."

Koh went to climb out. Paused upon sensing that Traeger wasn't following.

"Something wrong?"

Traeger's response was to dive into his pocket for a folded sheet of paper, which he spread and stared at repeatedly between fixations on the driver's bare back.

Which prompted Koh to drop her foot to face him.

"What is it? You look like you've seen the proverbial."

"It's the driver. From the back with that red hair and not much on, God she reminds me of the Streaker. Look."

Koh did.

"Really? Yeah, well ..." Screwed up her nose. Tilted her head. Raised her head to study the naked back on the dock. Back at the printout again. "This is pretty fuzzy and up close. Then again ..."

Raised her voice.

"Hey, honey. You with the tight buns sunning your boobies."

The driver didn't react.

"Hey you. Lady of the taxi driving persuasion."

The driver looked over her shoulder.

"You want me?"

"Yes, you."

The driver fully turned and squatted down dockside to talk close.

Robin duMerrick

"What's your name?

"Fran Mazzotti. What's yours?" Fired back.

"Jack the Ripper. So, Fran Mazzotti, by any chance was it you taking a dip in the bollicky in Elvina Bay a few days of last week or so?"

"In Elvina? In the nud? Too many houses. Beside, I wouldn't want Yodel to put his ferry on the rocks, now would I? Why?"

"It's just that someone did who looks like you from the back."

"Sorry. Wrong buns."

"You got any tats. On your right shoulder maybe?"

Mazzotti showed her shoulder.

"Shoulder, no. Where my tats are you need to donate a gold coin per squiz."

Koh pondered for a beat. She cast a look around to check they had Mackerel to themselves.

"Say, you wouldn't care to turn around and take off your clothes, would you? Just to knock the notion on the head. There's nobody else in the bay but us three. I've got a gold coin somewhere."

Traeger's face pinked. Mazzotti didn't turn a hair.

"What are you, Ripper, some sort of new-age lezzo?"

"I'm a cop."

"Then a new-age lezzo cop."

"It's my mate here. He's sure it was you he saw."

Mazzotti raised an eyebrow at Traeger.

"Trust me, I'd remember if I got it all off in front of this stud. So would he."

The pink turned a shade darker.

"Look I'm sorry I mentioned it, I ..."

"So that's a no? Even if it helps with a police investigation?"

Mazzotti chuckled.

"I thought I'd heard every try-on in the book to get

52

Streaker

me to drop my duds, but this is a newy." Hit on a new angle. "Say, if you're looking for a threesome, you'd have more luck giving me a call after I get off my shift. *Honey*."

Traeger hustled out of the cockpit and up alongside Mazzotti, who didn't step aside to give him room. He skirted her, avoiding her eyes. She was studying him closer than he liked.

"Excuse me if I bail. This conversation is getting ... *Phwoh*!" Said as if he was feeling the heat and didn't need to find the right word anyway for how the conversation was developing. "My mistake. Forget I said anything. Detective Koh, let's get on with it, shall we?"

He turned his back on them both and trotted off along the jetty toward land without checking if Koh followed.

Koh hustled onto the jetty alongside the driver. Mazzotti waited till Koh was close before whispering.

"How'd I do?"

"I'll let you know." Also in a whisper, before Koh hurried off after Traeger.

A head shorter than the lanky Traeger, she had to break into a near run to catch up with him. He didn't break stride. She fell in alongside at a brisk march. Tried not to puff as she spoke.

"She shone light into your black hole, didn't she. Tell me about it."

"She looked like the Streaker, that's all. The same colour hair. But no seahorse tattoo, right?"

She did her best to study his face for a reaction without tripping over her feet on the uneven boards of the jetty.

"So, nothing at all."

"No. Now you promised me a tour of your investigation, so let's get on with it. What next?"

She sighed and followed him to the end of the jetty.

53

There, he paused for her to catch up. Scanned left and right until she answered the question in his mind.

"We go right."

"To do what? I've seen it all before. I guarantee it hasn't changed since I was a kid."

She stepped onto land and started walking and talking. He followed.

"Remember me saying there was apparently only one party in Mackerel through Feb 6 and 7? The Dimitriou family?"

Streaker

10: Watchers

Fran Mazzotti leant back on her boat's coach-house, sunning herself. She had no reason to think that the blue flybridge cruiser standing five hundred metres off shore had any interest in her.

If she had been looking that way when the sun caught flare off the lenses of 12x50 field glasses, she might have wondered. If she had heard the words on the lips of the man behind the glasses, she would have worried.

"The undercover cop stayed with the water taxi. The other two are on their way."

He was speaking into a VHF radio held close to his mouth by a shorter, tubby companion in a terry-cloth bucket hat. The radio crackled with a garbled response, which he answered.

"Right. They went right. No, sir. Nowhere near the house. Just the same, is just as well the J-man heard about this."

The taller man with the binos was in his late forties. Wore a baseball cap, a bun of greying hair poking through above the adjusting strap.

On the flybridge dash in front of the pair, a Commodore's hat was shelved. On its front, "TOP

Robin duMerrick

COX" embroidered over an anchor.

"Sure. If they do, we'll take care of it."

Streaker

11: Hetty's place

Traeger chewed gum, hanging on Cassie Koh's every word as the pair marched along the track north in front of the cottages.

He was barely aware of their passing the bow an old 30 foot deep-keeler on a hardstand between two cottages, propped on the wider, farside gap by three 4x2 timbers jammed upright under the gunwale.

Barely registered the 44-gal drum, rusty paint scrapers on it, by the boat's bow, which was scraped clean of growth. Ignored the unlit street light on a pole on the right of their path opposite the keeler.

"The Dimitrious had spent a week here. The Monday night Fallon became a floater, they heard the water taxi come and go about the time they went to bed."

They were near the north end of the row of cottages. Koh stopped at an oldtimer. White-painted fibro, water tank at the side. A shark hook and "CAPTAIN HOOK'S CASTLE" on the door. Back against the wall, a rickety bench seat.

"You recognise this?"

It pulled him up. He back-pedalled to where she was gesturing. Screwed his eyes up at the ramshackle building.

"Should I?"

"Maybe you remember a girl pestering you to take her crabbing. A twelve-year-old by the name of Hetty Dimitriou. Does that ring a bell?"

"No." A sudden frown. "Why are you asking me this?"

"She's now dead, some say murdered. A year ago when I was working Homicide. In Bondi. I was pulled off the case ... But that's another story I'll tell you about some other time."

"What makes you think I'd know her?"

"Because she says so. Hetty kept diaries. All her life, as it turns out."

Koh sat on the bench seat. Slipped a red-bound, clasped diary out of her bag. Opened it at a bookmark. Proffered it.

"Read the passage I highlighted. And note the date: Feb 6."

He sat. Read.

"'Dear Diary, Hetty is upset. Danny sent her home. Sneaking out to go crabbing with Danny wasn't so bad really'." Annoyance flared up. "What sort of nonsense is this? She's writing about a 'Danny' not me."

"Danny, Denny, Dinny, Donny. Maybe to a twelve-year-old they all sound the same."

"Left field isn't far enough away to belt *that* ball."

"You don't recall paddling across to Mackerel from Palm Beach around that time to show a kid desperate for a big brother how to go catch crabs?"

He snapped the diary shut and shoved it into her lap.

"No I don't. Now can we get on with it?"

"What if I told you this 'Danny' knew Felicity Fallon and had the hots for her?"

"I'd say you'd given up being a cop to write plots for B-grade movies."

Streaker

"Okay. So let me read something in the diary that I *didn't* highlight."

She opened it and raised it to eye level.

"After the bit about going crabbing with 'Danny' she writes, 'What else? Oh, yes. Hetty thinks Danny is sweet on the taxi driver lady. Danny called her Felicity and looked sad. He said he wished she wouldn't squeeze his cheeks and call him her little man all the time. Hetty wishes Danny was keen on her like that. Maybe when she grows up and gets boobs he will. That's all for now. Big day. Sleep now and maybe Danny will paddle over again tomorrow and we'll go crabbing ...' Etcetera, etcetera. What do you make of that?"

"You're writing the B-grader."

Her lips firmed. Voice hardened.

"It sounds to me like 'Danny' hated that the woman he had a crush on treated him like a boy. Could be that sometime after Hetty snuck back under her covers that night to write her diary, 'Danny' came across Felicity somewhere. She patronised him once too often, he lost it, and he drowned her."

"You're not serious?"

"I bet you were a strapping lad at fifteen, what with paddling all over Pittwater. All that upper-body work in a boy developing into a man. You would've had the strength."

"Some damn detective. How many strapping lads do you think've paddled to Mackerel. Half my school did it at some time or other. And if I couldn't find a 'Danny' in the Old School Annual ..." He spat the gob of chewed gum into his hand and stuck it into her open diary page. "... I'll go pluck a duck. Are we done here?"

He marched off back the way they came, not caring if she followed. She picking gum off her papers to stuff in her bag while hurrying to catch up.

"Hold up, Tiger. I'm not done with you yet?"

59

Robin duMerrick

He spoke over his shoulder, not breaking stride.

"Oh, yes you are. If you don't want to swim, you'd better hustle your butt back to the taxi. Because, if that's the best you have for me on the Fallon case, I'm out of here."

Streaker

12: Boss cops

Koh entered the squad room, crossed to her desk and slipped her bag off her shoulder. She had her coat half off, ready to drape it over the back of her chair, when she felt a touch on her shoulder.

She turned, eyebrow raised at Lowe, the civilian police clerk.

"The Boss is trying to get your attention, Cassie."

She swivelled her head to peer through the glassed-off office at the two men there.

The one standing behind his desk, beckoning her, she expected. The other sitting in the visitor's chair before the desk she did not.

Which caused her nose to wrinkle.

The man behind the desk was her boss: Superintendent Dave Trumble. In his mid fifties. Smallish, buzzing with energy. Bushy grey brows, unruly grey-tinged hair. In a white shirt, sleeves rolled up, tie loose.

The other was Superintendent Stefan Juric. Late sixties. A bear of a man, jowly, with spare mousy hair brushed forward. No eyebrows. Large hands. Blue double-breasted suit, a darker blue shirt, a white tie, Windsor knotted big.

Robin duMerrick

Koh nodded okay at her boss and finished draping her coat on her chair before marching off to his office. Opened the door and stuck her head in. Didn't glance at Juric.

"Yes, Boss?"

"What? You can't spare a 'hi' for your old chief?"

This from Juric. Her response lacking enthusiasm, which didn't seem to bother Juric.

"So ... hi. How's everyone at Homicide?"

"We're all peachy. Missing you, of course. Particularly myself."

"Yeah, I'll bet." Then to her boss. "You wanted to see me?"

Trumble tried to ignore the static.

"Juric came here to find where we're going with the Fallon case."

Koh rolled her answer around on her tongue.

"Let's say we've turned up some promising fresh leads."

"Such as?"

"What's your interest, may I ask?"

"We in Homicide would like to know if we missed something back then. A matter of professional pride, don't you know."

She dropped belligerence for faux surprise.

"That's *ri...ght*." Drawn out. "You were on that case as a detective sergeant all those years ago, weren't you. Sir."

"Ha! Always the leg-puller. You know I was. It's all in the casefile."

"Yes, I recall being mystified reading you holding out for death by misadventure in contradiction to your partner at the time. Peter ... er."

"Masson."

"Masson. Right. Ex-Navy. Who pointed out that, windless, all floaty things drift with the current at the

Streaker

same rate. So why were Fallon and her water taxi found so far apart?"

"The key word being 'windless'. Meteorology wasn't what it is today. The Met boys couldn't swear that a breeze didn't spring up *sometime* through the night."

"And I noted you didn't follow up with all those folk staying in the bays that night."

"Dead end. No motive. But good try." Juric grinned at his Cold Case counterpart. "You see, Trumble, that's why she will make a damn fine investigator some day. Sorry to lose her to you, I truly am. She's like a dog at a bone. Doesn't give up on a theory even if her peers have buried it six feet under."

"Damning with faint praise won't get me to give her back." Grumbled, with wiry eyebrows low.

"Wouldn't think of it. Although then there is that mystery strategy I hear you've let her embark upon, Trumble old chap. Targeting a nutter who may know something about the drowning but who has forgotten it. Ha! Perhaps you could unravel that a little. It sounds like a time-waster to me."

She shrugged. Answered for her boss.

"I won't bore you with the details. It could be someone with a guilty conscience or simply someone who was there that night and saw the whole thing. A witness *you* failed to find was in Mackerel that evening."

"Mm. A senator's press secretary, they tell me."

Koh stared at her ex-boss blankly. Juric followed up.

"Well, let me tell you, young lady, you had better tread carefully. The senator is not a man to be trifled with."

"Is that a threat?"

"From me? Good heavens, no. But Arthur Candy does have the ear of the Deputy Commissioner. If he

Robin duMerrick

believes his people are being harassed, Candy will use his influence to bring heat down on all of us. Me included, if I failed to apprise you of the fact."

Juric stood, straightened his tie, eyed the other two.

"Which — having done my best to do — is my cue to bid you good day."

He extended his hand.

"Trumble."

He shook. Nodded at Koh.

"Detective Sergeant."

Turned and marched out.

Koh's eyes followed Juric through *Detectives*.

"How do you suppose he knows so much?" Idly aside to her boss.

"No idea. But he did say he found it odd that you signed out diaries you'd discovered in the closed Dimitriou case to revisit a seventeen year-old drowning."

"Mm, I doubt he was aware the Dimitriou diaries spanned two decades. In which case I don't see how he could make the connections I did. You didn't let on what we're up to?"

"Only that it involved a lot of manpower. But I said I've been prepared to give you your head for ten days before pulling the rug. Which has been whittled down to ..." Consulted his watch. "One day, two hours and thirty seven minutes as we speak. So I suggest you get about proving my faith in you is not misplaced."

Koh blinked and hustled to the door.

"Yes, Boss. I won't let you down."

"See that you don't."

Koh opened the door. Was about to step out when Trumble's recollection held her up.

"Oh, by the way, our Dr Laura called while you were out. She wants you to call her back."

Streaker

13: I had a dream

"You don't seem too disturbed by it? Aren't you sitting, Denny?"

From her power-chair, Dr Laura Schebel gestured Denny Traeger into his proper seat for interviews. But he remained standing behind the lounge, leaning on its back, pointing for her to pay less attention to him and more to the sheet of lilac notepaper and the fold-creased Streaker printout he had demanded she study.

"It was bound to happen. I'm not staying. I only wanted to give you the news."

She waved the note.

"It's obvious from this that she found the printout of your nude swimmer at home. Explaining to her that it was not a lover might bring your wife back."

"No. Our life together was a sham. My fault entirely. Her father was right. Shanta deserves better. In a way it's a relief no longer having to worry over a limp libido. Like maybe I no longer need a shrink."

"Denny, I urge you not to stop therapy at this crucial juncture."

"Just kidding. If you're determined to reinstate my status as a stud, who am I to argue?" He straightened. "Well, I've got to get to the office. Lots to do."

65

Robin duMerrick

He turned, turned back.

"Oh, there was one thing. This dream I'm having."

"Dream?"

"About Yodel. With repeats."

"The ferry driver?"

"Yes, In it, I ask him how come he never sees the Streaker. He tells me to shut up. 'I'm the top cox around here,' he says. 'You're just a bloody passenger'."

"Cox. That's the little man with a megaphone who shouts instructions at a rowing crew, isn't it?"

"Right. And Yodel is wearing this Commodore's hat. You know, like the rich wankers do to show they're top dog on board their luxury water toys."

"So, you are being reminded that Yodel ... or whoever he stands for in your dream ... is in charge. Why, do you think?"

"You're the shrink. You figure it out. In the meantime, I've got a press conference to organise."

Streaker

14: He had a dream

Schebel tugged the sleeve of Koh's jacket to pull her to the side of the corridor to let a gurney speed by with a gibbering patient strapped to it, pushed by a grim-faced orderly.

"I know I called *you*, Cassie, but I can only spare a minute."

"My bit will only take a minute."

"So?"

"Our victim lookalike didn't shake anything loose in close-up from him as we'd hoped."

"You have to give it time to sink in. Assuming ..."

"You still think I'm wasting my time."

"It doesn't make a difference to me either way. Right or wrong, your probing could open the Pandora's box that *is* my concern, even if it doesn't help your case."

"You still believe it was this Charlene who shut Pandora's box in the first place? Her rape?"

"That, I think, turned the key. It was his mother who lowered the lid over years of bellowing at him every time his father disappeared into the cellar with one of the bar girls." Then, seeing Koh's reaction. "He didn't tell you that? Apparently she would take it out on Denny, screaming the usual about all men being pigs

... and to watch himself or he would grow up a pig like them all."

"Nice."

"More than enough for him to become conflicted about his emerging sexuality. Reading his natural feelings — and particularly his feelings for Charlene — as sure signs he was turning into a monster like his father. I believe he has been fighting himself all these years with it. Until the news about his father raping Charlene shut the lid on it and threw away the key."

"Mm. But maybe, before it did that, it tipped the scales the other way. Into monster-hood. Like if a certain lady taxi driver got his temperature rising, along with something else."

"I'm sure you'll be proven wrong."

Her eyes on Koh, the shrink suddenly wedged the clipboard she was carrying under her armpit, freeing her hands to gently grip the detective's upper arms.

"You look tired, Cassie. You should take more care of yourself."

"I'm good. It's just that the whole thing has taken so much of the Department's manpower and time that I'm having to fend off some tough questions."

"Of course, if you have to call it all off, I will understand completely."

"No, we've gone this far. I intend to finish it."

Koh detached herself in the process of eyeing the progress of a tall suited man with grizzled hair and a stethoscope at his neck scurrying by.

"You do this stint every week *pro bono*, your secretary said. That means 'free', huh?"

Shebel nodded, her eyes still showing concern for Koh.

"Cool. Then I'll be sure to claim my discount when this case drives me nuts." Then: "But you called *me*, remember?"

Streaker

"Yes.I wanted to bring you up to date about his wife leaving him, and a weird dream of his. About a hat."

Robin duMerrick

15: Test

The Traeger living room had been stripped of all Indian furnishings. Little left other than the bar, the sound-system sideboard with its Bocelli collection, Traeger's trophies, fishing photo and Walkley Award.

Traeger stood — apparently unconcerned by the sparsity — reading a DVD jacket. Dressed in olive baggy cargo shorts and a pale green fine linen grandpa shirt, bare feet. A Cinzano soda on the sideboard, which was the only one of two horizontal surfaces left in the room other than the floor.

From the sound system, Andrea Bocelli was singing the opening lines of *The Prayer*.

Let this be our prayer … when we lose our way … Lead us to the place … Guide us with your grace … To a place where we'll feel safe.

Traeger dialled Andrea down to near mute at the ring of the door bell.

He went to the front door. Opened it. Blinked when he saw his visitor.

"Don't tell me. One of the police launches was free. Or did you catch a ride with my Streaker lookalike?"

Cassie Koh wore white jeans and a white camisole, not quite opaque enough to hide she wasn't wearing a

Streaker

bra. She had ditched Brooks walkers for unlaced fashion tennis shoes.

"Taxi. The Wateries frown on running off-duty cops about on private business."

"Is that what this is? Private business?"

"It would be if you let me in."

He hesitated, but then stepped back for her to enter. He followed her into the living room.

She took her time looking over the place. Poked a toe into two of the many impressions in the carpet where some antique furniture once stood.

"Nice address. But by the looks, lacking a woman's touch."

"A recent development."

"I'm sorry. And not just for that. It's why I came. To apologise. When it comes to my job, I'm a bit pushy. I know that.

"Forget it. I overreacted. It's my shrink. She's got me seeing ulterior motives under every stone. Drink?"

She pointed at his.

"What's that?"

"Cinzano soda."

She nodded. He moved to the bar and began to mix. She wandered around. Stopped at his trophies. Fingered his Walkley.

"You remember today wondering if you were being hit on by a cop? Well, maybe you were."

"That might be flattering if I had a libido that knew how to handle being hit on."

"You worry me, Tiger. You know that?"

He handed the drink to her.

"I worry me, too, if it comes to that. Here."

She sipped.

"Do you have something against us oriental types? I admit I don't have to beat them off with police batons, but some men have been known to fall over themselves

71

in their rush to fumble for a tumble. Not you. Not with me, anyway."

"I thought it was like drinking. You know, 'Not while on duty, thanks'."

"I'm not on duty now."

Koh put down her glass. Unbuttoned her cami, shrugged it off and dropped it. Traeger stared. But it wasn't lust in his eyes.

"My God, you look like a boy. Put your shirt back on."

Koh didn't look a bit hurt by the remark. Rather as if she half expected it. She made no move to cover up.

"I know I'm no double D-cup, but I can do things with these pointy bits that'll have you baying at the moon."

A sudden shrewd notion flitted over her face.

"Or does the boy-look turn you off."

An even shrewder thought when he averted his eyes.

"Or does it turn you *on*?"

He grabbed up her top and threw it at her.

"You'd better go."

She caught the top and began to put it on.

"Sorry. My mistake for thinking I had a lick of sex appeal."

"You know I have a problem in that department."

"Apparently. Let's forget it. Keep it strictly business between us from now on. Which is why I really came. I need your help with something."

"To do with the Fallon case?"

"To do with the Fallon case."

"What?"

"I need a guide. Tonight. Are you up for it?"

"Tonight? Why?"

"You'll see. We meet at Mitchell's Boat Hire at eight. Bring a torch."

Streaker

16: Night plan

Laura Schebel in tight shorts and stretch-fitting sports shirt was even more of a knock-out than in the tailored business suits she wore in her rooms.

Cassie Koh tutted her admiration as she walked up to the wire and hung fingers in the mesh, to the repeated whack of balls.

The courts were synthetic grass in two-tone green. Schebel was the player nearest Koh. The shrink's deep back bend, shoulders twisted way past side on, her left arm straight to the last moment in the ball toss, and uplaunch into the serve, told Koh that Schebel was no beginner.

As did the way the receiver didn't get her racquet to the ball.

Schebel called the score.

"Game. Set. Thank you, ladies."

The players ran to the net to shake. Walked to the sidelines to pick up towels and gear. Schebel saw Koh as she was towelling down. Smiled a greeting and came to the gate.

Koh pushed the gate inward with one hand, ushered Schebel through with the other holding a folder.

"Not bad. Remind me to challenge you ... to

Robin duMerrick

tiddlywinks. We need to talk."

Shebel's smile developed a rueful twist on one side.

"Let me guess. Denny Traeger. We can speak freely over here."

Schebel led Koh to the nearest gazebo. They entered, shutting down the volume on the patter of balls. They sat close. Koh passed the casefile to Schebel, who read, puzzlement spreading on her face.

"This is another Cold Case altogether. What has this to do with my patient?"

"Maybe nothing. Maybe something. Listen, I wanted to see for myself if Tiger couldn't get it up or was it an act. The reaction I got was a little weird. Me getting naked turned him right off."

Schebel shook her head slowly, her smile soft on the lady policeman.

"Is there *anything* you won't do to solve a case?"

"Maybe it's that I'm just not his type. On the other hand, I've never met the guy who'll turn down a snack-pack even if he'd rather have more fat on the cold cuts." Koh reflected briefly. "It was the way he reacted. As if I reminded him of young boys and it frightened him."

"Frightened him?"

"Yeah. As if he hated what he was feeling. In my time, I've come across rock-spiders who act the same."

"Rock-spiders?"

"Prison slang for paedophiles."

"Oh."

"As if they're scared shitless of not being able to control their urges."

"You think Denny Traeger is a paedophile?" Incredulous.

"Repressed, maybe. Fear that he might be turning into the sex monster his mother told him he'd become, like you said."

"On the strength of this?" Flapping the folder.

74

Streaker

"Did you read the date? Seventeen years ago. The kid was found raped and strangled up a backwater the other end of Pittwater the same morning Felicity Fallon was pulled from the drink with shrimps settling in for a snack."

Schebel's voice showed incredulity rising.

"So you think that, at fifteen years of age, my patient turned monster enough to drown a mature woman he fancied up one end of Pittwater and went looking for an prepubescent boy at the other end of Pittwater to rape and murder? And another mature woman taking a nude swim today stands to bring this extraordinary crime wave back into the forefront of his conscious mind?"

Schebel shook the file for Koh to take it back.

"What got you going on this anyway?"

"It landed on a co-worker's desk. The date and place hit me in the eye. Too much coincidence. So now I'm thinking 'solve one and I solve both'."

"Yes, well, I'm sure whatever is Denny Traeger's problem, it is not paedophilia."

The detective studied Schebel as if taking the opinion on board, before standing.

"Well, tonight we'll find out, won't we."

"And how do you propose doing that?"

"If I can't take him back to the scene of one crime I can at least do it for this one."

Schebel lingered over the sight of Koh's slim-boy back retreating down the concourse between the half dozen courts either side.

The psychiatrist opened her mouth to call after Koh to be careful but didn't manage it. She hadn't liked the sound of the detective's plan. Not one bit. But giving voice to unfounded fears was unprofessional.

Robin duMerrick

17: Sitting ducks

The rhythmic dip and splash was a sound eddy on the dark silence.

A wall of tangled bushes and trees overhung the black water.

Out of the gloom a dinghy appeared. Two figures hunched, one bent to stubby oars, the other in the thwart aft with a torch shining into her lap.

They wore topcoats and spoke in hushed tones.

The dinghy had a small outboard motor tilted clear of the water.

The torch lit a map and photograph in the woman's lap. She shone the torch on the map, then on the left bank, comparing one with the other.

Cassandra Koh.

"I see what you mean about rowing the rest of the way. How deep are we here?"

"In parts, just about deep enough for the prop to dig mud and bust itself on sunken logs if we hadn't tilted the egg-beater."

On the oars, Denny Traeger.

They rowed on, the headwater of McCarrs Creek narrowing.

"You really know your way around Pittwater. From

76

Streaker

one end to the other, eh?"

"When it's either fishing or hanging around a stinking pub, for a kid there's no contest."

Silence as they rowed on.

"Just the same, Tiger. Without you, I'd've been up shit creek ..."

"... without a paddle? And here I thought you didn't have a funny bone in your body."

"You didn't bother looking for one even when the body was on show, no gold coin, remember?"

He grunted noncommittally.

"You do remember I was no turn-on because of my boyish figure."

"You came on a bit strong, that's all. Can we drop it?"

"It's just that I should've warned you where we're headed is all about boys — if that's a sensitive topic for you."

"Boys? What's that got to do with Felicity Fallon's drowning?"

"There was another killing the same night. We think the two are connected. You wanted me to involve you in my investigation into anything to do with Fallon."

She shone the beam on his face. No reaction. She raised the photograph close to his face and directed the torch on it. He stopped rowing.

"Jesus. He couldn't be more than twelve."

He started rowing again. Squinted at the light in his face. She searched for a reaction, saw none. She swept the beam on as if lighting up his face was accidental.

A car cruised faintly in the distance. Its hum rose and fell as it negotiated a windy road.

"Eleven. Yeah, found the same morning as Fallon, right up the trickle end of this backwater. Hear that car? Way up there is the back road to St Ives. A track runs off it that kids use to get down to a clearing on the water

Robin duMerrick

where they do drugs. And the kid did have traces in him."

"So you're figuring the usual falling out among druggies."

"We thought that. Now don't. We reckon it was set up to look like it. The kid was strangled. Druggies knife each other. And the clearing didn't show any sign of occupation since the rains a week earlier. And then there was the anal scarring."

"The what?" Sharp in disbelief.

"And the drug was Rohypnol."

"The date rape drug?"

"Kids *do* do it recreationally. But we reckon he'd been drugged, abused and, when done with, strangled and dumped up this creek to look like a druggie."

She lit his face again.

The distant car hum suddenly died.

"Will you flash that thing on where we're going? It kills my night vision when you do that."

"Sorry. You didn't ask the kid's name."

"Does it matter?"

"You got around with the local kids. Maybe you knew him. Bari Khalib. Reported missing the day before, feared abducted outside his foster home in Fairfield."

"The other side of town. Nowhere near a local. So why would you think I'd know him?" The hiatus was in second thought. "Is there something here you're not telling me, Koh?" Annoyance in the tone.

A twig snapped way up the slope. Koh started in her seat.

"Shh. Did you hear that?"

"Stray dog. Water rat. Who knows? So how much further to this damn clearing? And what do you hope to find when we get there? And why're we doing it at night?"

Koh consulted her map again.

78

Streaker

"Not much further. I don't expect to find anything after all these years. To stage the drowning, Fallon's killer had to've had a boat. If he killed Khalib the same night, stands to reason he came here by water to dump the body and not by road. I just needed to check it was do-able. And do-able at night, moreover."

A twig snapped closer and bushes rustled.

She killed the light.

"And for mine, the matter's settled and it's time to get out of here. You hear that? Water rat or not, I'm spooked."

Traeger braked with the oars and begun to spin the dinghy around, in no particular hurry.

"You're the boss. I could've told you it was do-able without ..."

A torch beam more powerful than Koh's splashed across his face from up in the bush on the road side. The beam moved erratically, bouncing off trees. Someone was finding a way down through the bush.

"Who the devil ...?"

The someone was now crashing through the bush. A second torch beam splashed higher and to the left of the first. The someone spoke from up the incline.

"This way. They're down here."

Koh hissed her concern.

"I don't like the look of his. Can we get out of here?

Traeger finished the one-eighty. Dug the oars in hard. Koh had voiced his own thought, having caught glimpses of men through the undergrowth up the slope. And when the light beam in one pair of hands carved a fleeting moment over the other, Traeger saw that they were carrying something other than torches.

Which caused him to put his back into his rowing.

But not soon enough. The twin torch beams swept in from both ends of the stretch of headwater and intersected on their dinghy, and a voice from up there followed in swift demand.

"There, Rollo. Take your shot or they'll be out of sight." Shouted. A harsh voice in a North American accent.

Traeger reacted. Lunged at Koh. Grabbed her by the coat collar. Flung her into the centre of the dinghy. Took her place aft. Untilted the motor and yanked the pull-start. Yelled.

"Get the fuck down."

The motor revved, clunked into gear and screamed.

The *phut* before the ricochet confirmed to Traeger what their assailants had in hand.

Pistols. The sound said with suppressors. It also said to hunker as low as he could.

Koh stayed even lower. But it didn't mean she couldn't shout.

"I thought you said being shallow would fuck the prop."

"Does it look like I care?" Shouted just as loud, because now there was no point whispering.

Another *phut*. A clang into the aluminium transom. The propeller churned mud.

"Don't you have a gun you can shoot back with? You're a cop for Christ's sake?"

"We don't carry, normally."

She had raised her head and was fumbling her phone out. Stabbed its keypad.

"Normally! This is no normally. And don't waste your time. As mobile phone coverage goes, this isn't a dead spot, it's a black hole worse than my memory."

Two *phuts* in quick time. Another clang. Water spouts.

"And keep your damn head down. With luck ..."

The waterway ahead widened, a kink left. The dinghy took it. No more shots. Still hunched, Traeger glanced back. He got his voice back under control.

"They can't get a bead on us from here. Phew, what

Streaker

was *that* about?"

He slowed. They were between a wall of bush both sides.

The tiller suddenly shuddered in his grip.

"Oh, shit."

Koh checked over her shoulder before sitting up.

"What is it?"

Traeger cut the engine. Knelt on the stern thwart and tilted the motor. A chunk was missing from the prop.

"Told you so."

Koh understood the diagnosis immediately.

"Fucked the prop, right? Well I for one don't give a toss. Just get back on those oars and row us out of here in case those guys can find a way to put us in their sights again."

In the distance, a car started, revved. Traeger cocked his ear. Soon, the engine rose and fell in time with a tyre-squeal.

"Uh-oh."

"What is it now?"

He moved astern and grabbed her by the coat collar again to swap seats.

"Ow! Will you not do that?"

He plonked in the centre seat and began digging oars hard, at the same time, between strokes, straining to explain.

"That reserve we passed at the turn into this headwater. You might've noticed it from the dinghies stacked upright against poles there for yachties to get out to their moorings in the main channel."

"What of it?"

"If the shooters came down to the creek from the road, they drove there. That road finds its way down to the water right into the car park at that reserve. Listen."

Koh did. The tyre and engine song was louder. High

up, headlights strobed the trees, moving right to left, fast.

She grasped the urgency.

"Which means we've got to get past that reserve before they get there."

"And they say cops've got no brains."

"Shut up and row."

They were approaching the bend where the headwater turned sharp left at mangroves and reeds, into the main channel. The tyre and engine song had risen. Was suddenly too close for comfort.

To the fugitives' right, a large reserve opened out. Rustic tables. Public barbecue. Dinghies on end chained against upright poles. Closer to the road, a car park. A blue Caribbean 26 cruiser was tied to a stub jetty. No one was about at this hour.

"C'mon, c'mon. If we're not to hell and gone before they drive onto that reserve, we're sitting ducks."

He hadn't needed telling.

"We only have to ... get around this ... bend and among the ... swing moorings. Yachts'll ... give us cover. Unless ..."

"Unless what now?" But her anxious view over her shoulder told her that waiting for his answer was low priority. "Christ, here they come. Cut the damn corner. *Cut the damn corner.*"

A GT Ford fish-tailed into the car park. Skidded to a stop. Two men piled out, guns in hand, sprinted to the jetty. No sooner were they lined up, their target crossed in their torch beams, than they lowered their guns as their quarry rounded the mangrove bend out of sight.

Their faces—dimly lit in the backwash of their torches coming off a warning sign on the jetty—were contorted in fury. Their shadows betrayed one as tall, the other fat.

#

Streaker

A largish single shadow marked the slow-moving dinghy heading north in the main channel of McCarrs Creek. Two human silhouettes hunched in it, one alive in frantic action.

Right, a logjam of yachts sat sullen in the still night air on swing moorings. Dark homes hung off steep slopes further right. Left, Ku-ring-gai Park presented a brooding rampart of bushland.

Koh, in the stern of the dingy, had to look over her shoulder to check that the reserve was out of sight around the mangroves of the bend.

"We made it. Don't blow a boiler. They can't get at us here."

Traeger at the oars didn't let up.

"Unless ..."

"There it is again with that damn 'unless'. Unless what, damn it?"

"Unless that big cruiser you saw at that jetty is theirs."

A strong starter motor cackled behind them. A high-powered outboard revved and settled back to an idle.

Traeger cocked his ear, still digging hard.

"A Caribbean 26 with not one ... but two 220 horsepower outboards."

As if answering him, a second engine started, revved, idled.

"Either of which will cut us in two unless ..."

"Unless you think of something *fast*."

Traeger upped his stroke rate. She glanced back, the sight sending her voice sharply up-pitch.

"*Here they come, for Christ's sake.*"

With his back to the bow of their dinghy, her companion at the oars didn't need telling. He could see for himself the bow of the cruiser as it nudged into view from around the bend, its engines rising to a roar.

Desperation drove him to scan for sanctuary over

his left shoulder. Their only chance, to get lost among the moored boats, whose clutter in close quarters would slow the cruiser to a crawl.

He struck out for the nearest vessel, a fifty foot ketch with a clipper bow. He had twenty metres to go. The cruiser had a hundred. Five times as far. But, when up to speed, over five times as fast.

It came, still accelerating. Traeger strained. The clipper bow crawled closer. Traeger gauged. At best a dead heat. The cruiser flat out, threatening to seriously trim the margin. But once within the final ten metres, surely it would have to slow or risk not having room enough to steer clear of the ketch and almost certainly colliding with it.

Traeger was counting on it. He listened for the deceleration. It didn't come. Were they mad? He put every last breath into his strokes. Within five metres, the pursuers were still full bore.

Then he saw their sweep to port, steering a course to graze the ketch and wipe the dinghy off the map. He was within three strokes of being able to duck through the gap between the curve of the clipper bow and the yacht's anchor cable. The bow of the cruiser knifed the sea. It towered over them, it was so close.

Three strokes to go. Koh screamed. Traeger put every last muscle at breaking strain. Would it be enough? The cruiser bow seemed to be toppling onto them. They felt the pressure wave ahead of the powering hull. One stroke. The blue hull hunched its shoulders in one last lunge at them. Koh sank to her knees in the bottom of the dinghy, her scream piercing.

Traeger threw his head back to put everything he had into one last gasp to shoot the gap. The applied force levered him from his seat. The cruiser bow was within inches of ripping their small craft apart and swiping their bodies along the yacht's topsides like fish

Streaker

paste knifed onto bread.

#

Traeger slumped in the moon shadow against the moorings side of the ketch, chest heaving. He heard big outboards run on for no more than two seconds before they cut to idle. The wash of the sudden stop of the big vessel was as loud as a surf break.

"They know they missed us."

There was relief in Koh's voice, but not much.

The roar of opposing engines told the fugitives that the cruiser was being spun in its own length.

"They're coming back. Do something."

Traeger was still doubled, panting. He tried to straighten and failed. Tried again and managed the briefest appraisal of their options. His scan for escape bypassed an old riverboat and went on to a tar-black barge. He did a double-take on the riverboat.

The twin outboards grumbled just the other side of their hide. A searchlight swept the black water.

He started rowing again. Was careful to keep the ketch between him and their hunters. Headed for the barge. He had little breath to spare for explanations. Kept them brief.

"Hope you can swim."

"You're not thinking we can out-swim them!"

"No. Out-think them. "

The cruiser at idle had begun to nose into the moon-shadow side of the ketch where its quarry was moments before.

But by the time it had a clear view north and south in the second row of moored vessels, Traeger had ducked out of sight behind the barge on its channel side.

Koh wondered why he stood, holding onto the side of the barge. He seemed to be looking for something. Before she could ask, he dropped a keg-sized boat fender off at her feet. Then a second.

Robin duMerrick

He sat. Spoke in a whisper even though the grumble of the outboards on idle should've been enough to muffle normal conversation from that distance. Probably because that distance was becoming steadily less.

"Get your coat off." Then seeing her hesitate. "Off, off. Get forward. I need to be there."

She did it. The dinghy rolled and pitched with her movement, causing her to wave her arms for balance.

He let her cope. He was too busy wrapping a coat around each fender and zippering up each front. He sat the fenders upright together on the rear dinghy seat and lashed them to the tiller of the outboard motor with the ropes tailing both fenders.

"Over the side. Don't splash." Then hissed, sensing her reluctance. "*Do it.* Then pray there's enough life left in this prop."

Koh rolled into the water, not fully understanding his intent. She clung to the gunwale. Her shiver wasn't only for the sudden chill of the water wicking through her clothes.

She watched him carefully. He seemed to be sighting the bow of their dinghy back over the track they had taken from the mangrove corner. She flinched when he yanked the pull-start. The engine spluttered. He yanked again and she had a glimmer of hope he hadn't lost his mind.

#

High off the water, the two men on the flybridge should've had a good enough view over the dark vista to spot their quarry. Would've, but for the clutter of moored vessels spreading to their left and halfway to the mangroves.

They scanned left and right, the shorter of the two sweeping with a powerful searchlight mounted on the port side of the forward bulkhead.

Suddenly the sweep of the light stopped and swung

Streaker

back to seek the source of the piercing howl of a small outboard motor bursting into life. A blur of motion from the other side of a black barge provided the focus needed for the light to pinpoint the precise location.

A dinghy with two bulky shapes in the stern shot from the far side of the barge, heading back to the mangroves. In response, the tall man at the helm of the cruiser slammed the two throttle levers down and the big vessel leapt forward in pursuit.

#

The riverboat with *Swampy* on its transom dipped slightly at the stern as Denny Traeger emerged from the water and climbed the aft ladder. Big outboards roared far off. A small outboard howled even further away.

He helped Cassie Koh aboard, both dripping.

He ran his hand under the gunwale. It came out gripping a key. With, it, he unlocked the cabin door. Stepped aside for Koh.

"Inside. Quick. It won't fool them for long."

#

It was a no-contest. The little outboard couldn't possibly out-pace two big ones in a far bigger boat boasting a superior hull speed. The skipper of the cruiser had a grim smile on his face at the rate with which he was closing the gap.

But he hadn't reckoned on the course of his quarry. Its track was curving slightly right, not around the bend where the cruiser would certainly run it down, but short of it.

His smile wiped the second he saw he couldn't follow the dinghy where it was headed and had to pull the throttles fully back to watch helpless as the little vessel carrying the two shadow shapes speared deep into the reeds among the mangroves.

He let go the helm, leaving the cruiser to wallow in the catch-up of its speed wake. Snatched the .357 S&W

Robin duMerrick

off the dash, lined up the shadow shapes and let fly.

Phut, phut, phut.

The shorter man at his side followed suit, even more aggressively emptying his magazine at the same target. Fabric and stuffing flew off the two shadow shapes. Then rope, as its fibres were, by chance, severed by the volley. Which let the two human-like forms slump apart, the right one falling forward, the left one canting over the port gunwale and shedding its coat, revealing its true form.

"*Fuck.*"

With a roar of engines, the tall man spun the cruiser with opposing engines and set a reciprocal course at search speed.

"*Fuck, fuck, fuck.*"

The chubby man said the obvious.

"Back at that barge! They must've taken to the water."

"Shut up and sweep with that spot. Every fucking inch of this fucking waterway."

#

Koh leant with her back to the door and appraised the cabin. The space before her ran the full length of the narrow-beamed vessel. There was no "below decks". The foc's'le was open. The only space with a door was clearly the head, not big enough to hide two.

Far off, big outboards grumbled.

She noted the helm position was inside to her right. Behind it, a chart table. On the port side a galley and what she took to be a double berth because of the way it was made up.

That was until Traeger strode forward and stripped the blanket off to reveal the mattress in three sections, the outer ones seat width. He dumped the pillows and larger cushioning before lifting a centre panel. Clipped one end of it into the wall at table height and dropped a

Streaker

hinged leg to prop the panel level.

A dinette convertible to a double bed.

He spoke as he stowed the pillows into the lockers under the bench seats. Picked up the blanket and passed it to her.

"Get those wet things off."

He pulled out a wad of folded towels from under the other seat locker.

"All off. Dry yourself. Thoroughly."

She shook her mobile taken from her wet jeans. Wiped it. Pressed the "on". Put it to her ear.

"Don't waste your time. Believe it or not, the coverage here gets worse after you take your phone for a swim. Now, strip. *Fast.*"

She hesitated but did so upon seeing him get started doing the same. She towelled down. Wrapped the blanket around her.

He saronged his towel, glanced at her, frowned.

"Feet. Dry them too. Any wet spots will give us away."

He headed for the door with a fresh towel. Opened the door, letting in a louder grumble of 440 horses.

\#

From the flybridge of the cruiser, the spotlight scanned ahead into the moored boats, the big outboards grumbling on dead slow.

"They could've gotten onto one of the boats."

The taller man built on the fat man's conjecture.

"They'd have to break in. Scan for broken locks. Every goddamn boat we pass." Another thought. "And anything wet above the waterline."

\#

Traeger was on his knees where they had come over the stern, mopping up as he backed into the cabin.

Koh, just inside the door looking out, cupped a hand to her ear. Decided that the grumble of big engines had surely grown louder.

"I think they're heading back."

"Yep."

"You think they might look in here?"

"Yep."

#

From the flybridge, a fat hand worked the spotlight from left to right. The light beam swept over the black barge, came back and locked onto it.

"That's where we lost them. Betcha."

"Then we'll search every boat within a moose's holler of it. And all the water in between. We've got to find them."

#

The white beam knifed through the night, dicing the dark into discrete chunks.

Koh ducked as the beam splashed the windows of the riverboat. The grumble of the big outboards had grown even louder.

"They can't fail to see us."

Traeger was too busy at the double bed, finishing off rearranging it back into its dinette role.

When he was done, he grabbed her arm to pull her closer.

"Get in under. Tuck your legs up. Leave space for me."

She understood his plan. She turned, dropped to all fours and backed in, got her tail tight against the inner skin of the hull and drew her knees up to her chin.

Traeger had also gone down on his knees. He was mopping the wet spots they'd left on the cabin sole.

Koh watched, wondering why he had stood again. With a cut-off view of just his lower body she could only guess he was checking his handiwork.

He stooped below the line of windows as the spotlight scythed over them briefly. The moment it

Streaker

moved on, he snatched up towels and clothes, opened the door to the head, threw them inside. Left the door open so the searchers could see there was no one hiding in there.

Then he joined her under the table, aware that the big cruiser was now very near.

"Move over."

The two huddled together. Light swept their hide, held on them, flickered. Their world vibrated with the rumble of the big outboards. Then, ominously, the rumble died to out-of-gear idle.

Koh stiffened and clutched Traeger. He put his arm around her and hugged her close. They held their breath. The spot—as glaring as white-hot steel—slowly tracked down the floor, passing mere inches from their toes, which they pulled back in a desperate cringe.

The moment seemed to last, with another sweep of the light on the floor. Then the idle stepped back up to power rumble and the dark returned. Only an occasional flash of stray light reached them as the search resumed.

Koh let herself breathe again.

"They're moving on."

"We're staying right where we are until we're sure they're gone."

"If it takes all night?"

"If it takes all night."

They fell silent. After a while he felt the tension begin to ease from her body and was glad of it.

"Like this?"

"Like this."

Their faces were close. She, under his arm, looked up into his face. Half smiled. He looked down at her.

"That's okay by me. Except ..."

"Yes?"

"The top half of me is comfortable. Very comfortable. But my leg is getting a cramp."

"Well stretch it out. But you'd better pull it back in before you fall asleep in case they do a second pass."

She snuggled her head into his shoulder.

"You think I'm going to sleep?"

"Stress does that to some people."

"Who's stressed? I told you, I'm as comfy as can be."

"It's okay. If you do, I'll pull your leg in for you. Consider it fair exchange for getting me shot at. Now be quiet. I need to hear when they give up on us."

"Yes, I need to hear that too." Drowsy. Then a second thought. "How did you know where to find the key?"

"I've known Swampy since I was a kid. He taught me how to tie a bowline."

"Be sure to thank Swampy for me."

"Sure. How's that cramp?"

"Doing well, thank you. Will you let me know, Tiger, mm?"

"Let you know what?"

"When they're gone. Will you? Mm?" Slurred.

"Sure."

Her leg unfolded itself out from under the table as she relaxed into sleep. The rumble of the cruiser's twin engines has fallen off with distance. Traeger stared at the bare leg as it unravelled from her blanket wrap.

He gently re-covered her leg as best he could.

Streaker

18: Morning after

The dinette had been made up into a bed again. Its blanket covered Cassie Koh to the neck. Soft morning light touched her face, shifting gently as the vessel swung on its mooring. The sea lapped on the hull in a liquid lullaby.

The sizzle of something in a frying pan stirred her. Her nose twitched. Her arms stretched out from under the blanket. Suddenly, her eyes snapped open, puzzled.

Denny Traeger stood fully dressed by the gas range, shaking something in a frying pan. Past him, the door to the cabin was latched back, giving a view of flat blue water strewn with masts. Halyards tapped out a tinny Morse code on the masts under the strum of a gentle breeze.

Her eyes move to the cord strung across the cabin, all her clothes hanging. She lifted the edge of her blanket. Looked down her naked length. Pulled the blanket back to her chin.

"Yeah, right."

He look around at her questioningly, still shaking the pan.

On the counter was a packet of crackers, an egg

slide, half a bottle of olive oil, a knife on a cutting board, two plates, two forks and two mugs. On a lit gas ring alongside the frying pan was a coffee percolator.

"At last. I told you stress makes sleepy-heads of some people."

"And makes pervs out of others. How did I go to sleep papoose-wrapped in a blanket and wake up not?"

"There was only one blanket. It got cold. I didn't think you'd want me to freeze."

"So from me being blanketed alone, to you and me being blanketed together, you must've got to see me not blanketed at all, right?"

He shrugged.

"When I tried to show you my wares myself, you went all coy on me. What was different this time?"

"You didn't give my eyeballs a chance to pop themselves back in the first time, that's all."

"So when you can take your time getting an eyeful, I look less like a boy and more like a woman, is that it?"

"Something like that. I hope you like fried cheese. Swampy's always got some Haloumy on board. His name is actually Nikos Papangellis."

"So if you've already seen it all ..."

She flipped off the blanket and rolled off the end of the bed.

"... why am I waiting for you to preserve my modesty by passing me my clothes blindfolded? Which I assume are, by now, dry."

She pulled her clothes off the line. Pretended to ignore his glance.

While she dressed, he slid the fried Haloumy onto each plate with the egg slide, added some crackers, poured two coffees and juggled the lot as he stepped through the door into the cockpit outside.

"No silver service, but breakfast is served."

Streaker

#

The cockpit had sprouted an extra feature since she saw it last. An erectable outside table had been fitted between the fore-and-aft seating of the cockpit, the far end clipped into a bracket on the transom and a fold-down leg supporting its near end.

Koh stood in the cabin, her face jutted from the companionway to peer left and right uncertainly at the moored vessels around them.

No one aboard any of them. No rumble of big engines.

Assured, she turned her attention to her companion placing their breakfast plates onto the table as he slid into the seating. He picked up his fork and took his first mouthful.

Only then did she come on deck.

"They gave up, huh? Eventually?"

She wriggled into the seat opposite Traeger.

He sipped coffee.

"About two in the morning."

She tugged at the table. Solid. He forked in some Haloumy.

"What is it with this boat and tables, anyway? Last night this wasn't here, now it is. The one in the cabin was a table and now it's a bed. Which reminds me, where did you put me ... blanketless, I might add ... while you converted the table we hid under?"

"On the floor." He read the need to respond to her frown. "On one of the seat cushions. Until I could lift you onto the bed made up." Read a little deeper. "With a towel over you. To preserve your modesty." He pointed at her plate. "Eat before it gets cold."

"Gallant of you. Even if, in the end, the sleeping arrangements were somewhat conjugal. What with both of us being naked under the same covers and all."

She picked up her fork and tried the Haloumy with

95

Robin duMerrick

no hint of enthusiasm ... at first.

"Hey, not bad this."

He picked up a cracker and munched on it.

"If you're worried did I take advantage of the situation ..."

The way he let it hang caused her to arrest her fork halfway to her mouth. But he had more to let hang.

"I have to be honest ..."

Her face showed doubt before she seemed to make up her mind and let the fork go to her mouth.

"No. I'd know." Emphatic.

Finished, he put his fork on his plate and reached for his coffee. But his eyes, serious, didn't leave hers.

"At first I thought, 'Denny my man, confound your mother's opinion that all men are pigs. Do the decent thing'." Manner serious, dropping suddenly to lascivious. "Then I said 'Why fight it. After all, she tried to seduce you. It's only fair,' I said. Sooo ..."

She fumbled her fork. It clattered onto her plate. She studied his face. Absently, she picked her fork up again, poked at her food, distracted by his scrutiny.

"You didn't. I mean, I didn't. That is, about me seducing ... Not really. I was just testing ..."

His eyes lost their humour. Became sharp with suspicion.

"Just testing what exactly?"

"I ..."

"It has something to do with getting me to take you up that backwater last night, doesn't it?"

"No. I ..."

"Another test. After the striptease to show me a body like a boy's. To see if I liked bodies like a boy's, maybe? Yes?"

"But you didn't. Just the opposite. I'm sorry I ..."

"No you're not. You've graduated me from a killer of lady taxi-drivers to a kid-killing rock-spider. You

96

Streaker

think murderous paedophilia runs in my veins, for Christ's sake."

She looked sheepish. He reached across and grasped her wrist. Shook it so hard the fork clattered to the floor.

"*Admit it.*"

She bounced the agression.

"*I had to be sure.*"

He glared at her. She struggled to free her wrist. He held it in an iron grip for a beat, then suddenly let go. Stood and scooped up the plates and mugs.

"And I thought we were helping each other over the Fallon mystery. *Well, to hell with you.*"

He marched off through the door to the cabin.

Koh's face slumped. She fidgeted in her seat all the while dishes rattled inside, her mind in turmoil. Then she snapped herself out of it, reminding herself of her duties.

She had to raise her voice to make herself heard by the man stewing inside.

"Whatever you think of me, you have to find a way for me to contact my people. They'll need to go picking slugs out of trees up that creek. ASAP if we're to have a hope of finding who was using us for plinking practice, and why." And to a lack of reaction: "Do you hear?"

In answer, the riverboat's diesel engine started and was throttled back to a *putt-putt* ready to get under way as soon as the anchor was weighed.

Robin duMerrick

19: Police business

The Water Police base in Pittwater is on the second floor of the office, workshop, showroom and retail complex serving a recreational marina half a kilometre inside the mouth of McCarrs Creek.

The police precinct is cramped even for two officers. Two desks facing each other. Filing cabinets. Chart table. HF and VHF stations. Sink with coffee making. Lockers. Pegs hung with heavy weather gear and police caps. Charts of Pittwater, Broken Bay and Brisbane Waters on the wall.

The view is over the compact array of berths, mostly occupied by private vessels, to the main channel. Except at the end, where two outer berths are the domain of two police launches, one ocean-going, the other a power-cat for more protected waters.

Detective Koh was sitting at one of the desks, speaking into a phone, ignoring the view.

"We've just given our statements."

Her eyes were on two diaries, marked as such by the strap and key-holed clasps meant to keep a diarist's secrets secret. The keys lay alongside. The red diary was open. The other was identical except for being blue, and was closed but with a press clipping jutting from its top

Streaker

edge, bookmark-wise.

On a phone deeper in the room sat a uniformed officer, whose lapel badge identified him as Senior Constable Jason Temple.

The badge on a second uniform crossing the room from the coffee percolator announced *his* name as Constable Warwick Cobb

Cobb carried two steaming mugs. He approached Koh and put one of them to the right of the computer screen on the desk she was using. Koh's eyes met his for the time it took to nod thanks, but dismissed his attempt to begin any kind of charm offensive.

She returned to her phone conversation as if the young officer had been summarily vapourised.

"Where is he now?" This, tinny down the line from the other end. From the desk of Dr Laura Schebel in her rooms.

Koh lightly stroked the open page of the diary with an idle index finger as if using a highlighter on the passage her eyes were fixed on.

"Gone to wait for Swampy to turn up. That's the owner of the boat we hid in. He wants to explain borrowing it and go with the guy to put it back on its mooring."

"But you're now convinced he had nothing to do with the little boy's death seventeen years ago."

"I am. But I've found something that convinces me he did have something to do with Fallon's death."

"Tell me."

"When you get here."

"Who says I am going anywhere?"

Koh reached for the blue diary. Opened it at the press clipping. Took the newsprint out and stared at the head-and-shoulders of the man under the headline "SENATOR APPOINTS PRESSMAN". It was someone she knew. The man they were talking about.

Robin duMerrick

A phone rang somewhere behind her.

"You have to, Laura. He's already pissed at me. If I show him what I've found out without you here to soften the blow, I think it might blow his mind."

Senior Constable Jason Temple caught Koh's eye. He had his hand over the mouthpiece of the phone he was holding up.

"Hold on a sec."

She raised her eyebrows at Temple in a query he answered.

"The brass say they're five minutes away."

Koh nodded okay at Temple and turned back to her call.

"I'm back. Well?"

"I must say I am not delighted with your bumbling intervention in my patient's treatment. It almost got you both killed."

"I get that. But I did learn one thing."

"What is it?"

"Tiger is not as fragile as you think, shrink-wise. He was magnificent out there last night. Bloody magnificent."

She gave it a beat for that to sink in.

"Now promise me you'll come. I'll get one of the cops here to go find him with the news you called to tell him. He's not speaking to me right now ... Mm?"

She heard out the interruption.

"No you can't. His phone got as drowned as mine did in the melee. So I'll take it that's a 'yes'. But wear some sensible shoes. I've got a feeling we're going to need to take a boat trip."

Streaker

20: Swampy

Denny Traeger stood by the shelter on the ferry wharf. The riverboat named Swampy was tied alongside. He watched the ferry named Pegasus chug into the steps, to the faint sound of yodelling. The chug eased to an idle. The man named Yodel jumped ashore to tie up, ending his yodelling.

The first of the passengers off the ferry was lanky and bony. Bald. A broken nose, cauliflower ears, calloused brows.

His dirty black worsted trousers were belted with a length of rope. His checked shirt, open with buttons missing, showed a blue singlet and white chest hairs.

On his feet, tennis shoes so badly worn that one sole flapped and a toe peeked through.

He carried a brown duffel bag, gaping because its zip had stripped.

It was the man named Swampy after whom Swampy the riverboat was named. He muttered as he crossed the dock.

"Damn yodelling. Shouldn't be allowed on public transport."

Traeger stepped forward with his hand out. Swampy ignored it to look down at his riverboat. He dropped his bag. Jammed hands on hips.

"No bullet holes, you say."

"Not so much as a scratch. And I topped her up with diesel and replaced the crackers. The shop here doesn't sell Haloumy so I left enough on the galley top for you to buy half a ton of it."

Swampy turned to inspect Traeger with distaste. His head ducked and weaved as a leftover from his days boxing.

"You got fat. You were such a scrawny kid when I used to take you fishin'. If that's what getting married does, I don't want none of it. How'd you get shot at anyway?"

"Beats me. What I can tell you is that if it wasn't for the old tub, I'd be fish bait right now."

"I'd sure like to get my hands on the shitters who shot up my girl."

"You mean shooters. The police are all over it."

"Agh, the Wateries couldn't find a lost anchor cable if their props fouled in it. I say we jump in the good ship Swampy and go find them shitters ourselves."

Swampy's gnarly fists made tight feints near his face.

"Give 'em a round of the old one-two."

He air-swung two left jabs and a right cross.

"Cool it, oldtimer, you'll blow a stack."

"'N' if they won't stand and fight ..." He stooped and grabbed a sawn-off shotgun out of the duffel bag. Brandished it over his head. "... I'll give 'em some lead in the arse with my good old shotty."

"Christ, Swampy, put that fucking thing back in the bag quick. We're only a stone's throw from the Water Cop Shop for heaven's sake. If they see you waving that thing in public, they'll come and bust our balls."

Swampy stopped his jig. Looked a little disappointed. His arms dropped to his sides, the shotgun still in

Streaker

hand.

"Well, what did you get old Swampy over fer if it ain't to sort out them shitters?"

"To put your boat back on its mooring. You and me. Like the old days."

The old guy grunted. He shoved his shotty back in the duffel. Leapt to the deck of his riverboat. Not a trace of stagger despite the slight bob and weave of the deck.

"Well why didn't you say so?" Then seeing Traeger lagging. "Well, what are you standing there fer looking like a lump of liverfish? Get aboard."

"Can't. Not right away."

"What you got better to do?"

"Just give me half an hour. I've got a doctor coming all the way from town to check me out."

"I thought you didn't get shot."

"It's not that sort of doctor."

"Well I ain't hangin' about fer some scrawny kid I used to have to bait his hook fer."

Traeger took a hundred from his wallet and held it out toward the old man.

"Here, you old skinflint. By the time you restock your grog locker, I'll be done."

Swampy licked lips. Feigned reluctance but took the bill.

Robin duMerrick

21 : Boss cop flack

Koh tapped the keyboard connected to the computer on the Wateries' desk by the window overlooking McCarrs Creek

She blinked at the screen. Sipped coffee, still hot.

Suddenly she sat upright, her eyes wide. She stabbed the keyboard again, and four sheets of paper slid from the printer to the left of the screen.

Cobb moved in to sit sidesaddle on Koh's desk.

"You know, you need to wind down after all that bad shit. Whaddaya say? I'll be free at eighteen hundred. That's ..."

She didn't look up from the paperwork in her hand.

"Six o'clock. Yeah, I'm not only a hero, I can tell the time."

He tried another tack

"It's just that I see you're not attached. No ring."

"Gee, what a waste, you not working Detectives. Nothing gets by you."

Cobb reddened, stood, was about to say something when the door slammed back and two men marched into the room, Superintendent Trumble just ahead of Superintendent Juric.

Cobb went stiff upright.

Streaker

"Sirs, Constable Warwick Cobb at your disposal."

Trumble had already skirted him and Juric sent him sideways with a backhand swipe.

"Out of my way. Where is she? Ah, there you are, Koh. What do you mean by ...?"

But Trumble had beaten him to Koh's desk. She had risen, but he waved her back down, and gave his fellow Super his back in setting him straight.

"I'll handle this Juric. She's my girl now, not yours." Ignored Juric's blubbered affront. "You nearly got yourself killed, Koh. What in hell's name were you thinking?"

"Boss, you have to read my statement to appreciate ..."

Trumble shook his phone in her face.

"I had it emailed to me on the way here. Don't tell me what to appreciate, Koh. The case of the Khalib boy's strangling I personally assigned to Ted Gaston. What were you doing messing with it?"

"You know Ted's helping with my case. I offered to help with his. The date they found the Khalib boy leapt out of the file at me. It was the same day Felicity Fallon was making like shark bait."

That set Juric bull-roaring.

"Horseshit coincidence. That very same day my partner's wife dropped a kid. You might as well say Fallon's drowning broke Betty Masson's water."

"Two killings within hours of each other, on the same stretch of water less than five miles apart? That's some coincidence."

"Would be if Fallon hadn't drowned her stupid self, damn it."

Trumble cut him off.

"Butt out, Juric." Then to Koh. "So what? You suddenly pegged our Fallon suspect for the Khalib killing as well?"

105

She hesitated.

"A mistake, as it turns out." But then eagerly. "But it has taught me two things."

"What?"

"That I'm close to nailing the killers of both crimes."

"And the second?"

"That the rock-spiders we've forced out into the open are about to get fumigated."

Both Supers went stony-faced. But no one noticed the nervous tic that briefly inflicted an eye of one of them.

Streaker

22: Game plan

The tables at Pasadena's restaurant spread from inside to out onto the lawn, where they gave a two-seventy degree view of Pittwater. Four-man aluminium dinghies the locals call tinnies buzzed by under small horsepower outboards, to and from Scotland Island, Elvina Bay and even as far as Lovett and Towelers Bays.

Laura Schebel had taken a table outside where she could watch approaches through hotel reception. One approach in particular. Her patient, Denny Traeger's.

She didn't have long to wait. When he appeared, she rose and surprised him with a hug. Waved him into a chair.

"Thank God you weren't hurt."

"How did you find out?"

"I received a call from Detective Koh. She was equally as concerned about you. She insisted I come."

"Koh *knows* you?"

Schebel was hesitant.

"Denny, I've not been entirely open with you about all aspects of your ... treatment."

He narrowed his eyes.

"Oh?"

Robin duMerrick

She looked past him.

"Perhaps it is best coming from *her*."

He swivelled his head to see Koh crossing from the hotel foyer. She had her usual bag hung from her shoulder.

"Why do I get the feeling I'm being tag-teamed?"

"Hullo, Tiger. Ask me to sit, will you? You can't stay mad at someone you shared a bed with, surely."

"Shared a bed?" From Schebel, explained away by Koh.

"An in-joke. I'll tell you some time when we can look back on this around the campfire and have a good laugh."

"I thought I told you to go to hell."

"Denny, she was only doing her job. And she assured me she would consult with me every step of the way."

"*You* knew about it? Every step of *what* way?"

Koh took that.

"I twisted her arm. She had no choice but to cooperate."

"I don't understand. Are you saying you had me in your sights even before I came to ask you about the Fallon case?"

"I was going to bring you in for questioning until Laura here said that might send your buried memory even further into the black hole. She said you had to see your own way out of it. We gave it to you."

Koh pulled two diaries from her bag, one red, one blue.

"We? I don't understand. Before I came to see you, you couldn't possibly have connected me with the 'Danny' in that diary written seventeen years ago."

Koh brandished the red diary.

"In this red diary, no. But it was only one of the many that Hetty Dimitriou kept into adulthood. Including this one ..." Holding up the blue one. "In which she

Streaker

also gave you a mention, not long before she was found dead with her head in a gas oven."

"The case you were pulled off in Homicide, right?"

Koh nodded.

"Hetty edited *The Left Twist*, a city rag that got up the noses of the City Elders, politicians and the big end of town, including your boss."

"Candy? Not in my time."

"No, she was shut down just before you got on board. But it didn't stop her. She set out to write an exposé."

"Exposing Candy for what?"

"Somebody beat us to her laptop, office files or anything that would tell us exactly. Just an entry in her last diary, which we found with the others in a drawer in her kitchen. The same diary I found your name in."

"There must be some mistake."

"No mistake."

She opened the blue diary at the press clipping, which she passed to him. He studied the pic and headline.

"Mm. Me when I was appointed to Candy's staff."

"Now read the entry in the page the clipping bookmarked."

She passed him the open blue diary. He read.

"'Could this Denny be my Danny from all those years ago in Mackerel? Check it out.'" He frowned. "Well, did she or didn't she? Check it, I mean."

"We don't know. But of course *I* did. I traced your history back to Pittwater, which fitted. We watched you to be sure. Found out you were seeing a shrink. Were curious to learn if you might be suffering from a guilty conscience."

He handed back the diary and clipping.

"So much for doctor-client privilege."

"You've been watching too many episodes of *Law*

Robin duMerrick

and Order. If it's any consolation, I had to read the riot act for Laura to cooperate."

"Sorry, Denny. I had no choice."

By now, he had no patience for contrition.

"So, damn it, what've you two been cooking up between you exactly?" Suddenly hit by a thought, directing daggers at his shrink. "Hey, all this time you've been figuring I've been repressing a past as a fucking paedophile, too?"

"No, Denny. Not that. I ..."

Koh fielded it.

"That was strictly *my* brain snap I now know was off base, Tiger. Nothing to do with Laura. An afterthought on top of the original motive I hit Laura with of a crush on a lady taxi driver turned sour."

"*That*, I had to admit was a possibility. Or at least that you had witnessed the Fallon drowning. Quite sufficiently traumatic to trigger dissociative amnesia."

"Either way, I had to follow up on it. And confess I've been a believer ... right up till now."

"Because of someone taking pot-shots at us?"

"That and my re-read of the old red diary while waiting for my boss's debrief just now." She opened the red diary where its ribbon marked the page. "I was so fixated on the bit about Hetty's 'Danny' having a thing for the lady taxi driver, that I completely missed the significance of the rest of her entry that night. Listen."

Koh read, hamming up some of the child's spelling.

"'Dear Diary, Hetty is upset. Danny sent her home. Told her to sneak in the same way she snuck out, through her bedroom *winder*. So's her Mum and Dad don't know ever and not to *menshun* where she was tonight. Ever. Sneaking out to go crabbing with Danny wasn't so bad really. But it was something more than that, to do with what Danny saw in that house ...'"

"It's still a Danny. Not me." Angry and righteous in

Streaker

denial.

"Just listen. 'Danny was peeking in the *winder* but it was too high for Hetty to see in. Danny looked like he'd seen a ghost. He said we should never been there and had to get away from there quick. Hetty asked why but Danny didn't say. Hetty only heard music she didn't like. What else? Oh, yes. Hetty thinks Danny is sweet on the taxi driver lady.'" Reverting to her own voice. "And so on. You know the rest."

Schebel leant in. Put a hand on his. Searched his eyes.

"The point is, Denny, if Hetty's 'Danny' *was* you, what you saw through that window could have been enough to trigger that session of binge drinking and subsequent repression of it. Does the situation ring any bells at all?"

He chewed it over. Briefly.

"No. Sorry."

Koh exhaled audibly.

"Only one thing for it. We have to go there and find out."

"What? And peek in every window in Mackerel to see if I freak? You have to be kidding."

Koh took papers from her bag. Four sheets of copy paper. She shook them in their faces but didn't offer to reveal what they meant.

"No, I know which windows to look in. If you'll both trust me. Let me see if I can get the Wateries to take us."

But Traeger was shaking his head.

"No need. I just barely managed to hold Swampy back from scouring Pittwater for whoever dared to shoot up his playground that he'll jump at the chance to take us."

Then firmly. "Although I'm damned if I can see what good it will do."

111

Robin duMerrick

23: Reluctance

The sun was low. Koh, Schebel and Traeger at the end of the Mackerel jetty watched the old man fit an electric trolling motor to the transom of his riverboat.

The old man grumbled as he worked.

"I'm not twiddlin' my thumbs fer an hour if that's what you need. There were some kingies schoolin' just around the corner off West Head yesterdee. I'll take a pass or two trolling fer 'em and be back here before you get done. If'n I don't come across them shitters in the meantime. O' course, if'n you're early, you'll just have to wait."

"We'll be fine, you old skinflint. Go catch us some dinner."

They watched Swampy push off and set a silent course for the northern headland of the bay. He stood steering with the tiller between his knees while he rigged his trolling rods.

The trio started along the jetty.

At the land end, they paused while Koh consulted her papers. She pointed and led the way up the path into the shallow gully that Felicity Fallon took seventeen years ago.

Schebel followed a step behind. But Traeger

112

Streaker

hesitated, prompting Schebel to stop and look back.

"Is something wrong?"

Which prompted Koh to stop and look back.

He scowled at both of them.

"Nothing up that way but weekenders owned by the snooty and famous with waterfront mansions on Sydney Harbour but who hang onto the good old family summer shack the same way we plebs don't chuck comfy old tennis shoes. Rented, when they're occupied at all."

Koh hadn't heard all of it. Had other things on her mind.

"Are you two coming or not?"

Schebel's answer was to Traeger, not Koh.

"If so, there's nothing to be concerned about."

"Hey, I wouldn't mind getting home before midnight." Koh's voice rose out in front but ignored by Schebel intent on continuing her probe of her patient's agitation.

"Perhaps there is. Perhaps, Denny, this is a walk down memory lane. *Is* it?"

"No. Nothing of the sort."

"Then come along."

Traeger shuffled after her, mumbling as he unwrapped gum, popped it and chewed as a cover for his hesitancy.

"Damn waste of time if you ask me."

Koh's sarcastic take floated back to them on the wind.

"Oh, the mummy walks."

She waited for the other two to catch up. They continued up toward the brooding house.

24: The howl

Koh and Shebel moved onto the front veranda where Felicity Fallon had stood seventeen years ago. The house was in darkness. Schebel looked back at Traeger yet to step up, and beckoned.

Koh took a torch from her bag and shone it in the sidelights either side of the front door.

"Only furniture, covered. Like nobody lives here."

Traeger spoke up to them without moving.

"I've only ever seen light coming from the uphill side. Toward the back. I'd say nothing's changed."

Koh moved to the uphill side of the veranda and flashed her torch down the side of the building. She left Schebel to work her mind probe.

"Oh, so you know the place. Do you recall ever being here at night?"

"At night? I ... I shouldn't think so."

"Then how do you know which lights are usually on and which are off?"

"I ... I'm not sure. On weekends, there are lots of porch lights on all over Mackerel. I just have this image in my mind of this one dark."

Streaker

"Yet you know about a light coming from the rear ... on the high side."

"I don't know. I was all over this bay as a kid. Nights too, when the blue swimmer crabs were on."

"Sometimes sneaking a peek through windows, perhaps, Denny? Did you do that here? Into this house?"

"No." Emphatically.

"Not even out of curiosity? Wondering why the only light on in the whole place was at the back?"

"No. I said no."

"And on the high side, too, which is the only place where the slope of the block might let you see into a window?"

"I ... I don't remember." A moment's reflection. "I'm sure I didn't."

"Well, let's not guess. Let's see if that's even possible. Follow me. I'll light the way."

Koh had already set out along the gap between the house and a rising bank on her right hand side. Schebel herded a lagging Traeger.

The first window they came to was over man high. They moved along the rising ground. Koh arrived first at the second window. She shone a torch in through the window briefly before redirecting the beam to light the way for the others.

Schebel was next at the window. There was something about Koh's face that caused her to tense.

"What is it?" Whispered.

"Did you say something about a Commodore's hat featuring in that weird dream of Tiger's."

"Yes, why?"

Traeger caught up.

"What was that about me and dreams? Come on, what are you two cooking up now?"

Koh tugged his sleeve. Pulled him in front of

Robin duMerrick

Schebel.

"Stand close to the window, Tiger. I'm going to light it up for you and you tell me what you see?"

He hesitated. Stepped up. Stared into the dark. Suddenly her torch lit it up.

Against the far wall was a double bed. The door was open in the far left corner. An ancient free-standing wardrobe was against the wall on the right.

Just inside the window, right, on a table, sat a Commodore's hat all by itself, the front embroidered with "TOP COX" overlying an anchor, staring him in the face.

Traeger went into shock. Shadows flickered in his eyes as if he saw someone his companions couldn't moving in the room.

Koh and Schebel could only guess what was happening behind the horror-stricken face backlit by the torch.

They couldn't hear with his ears the heavy-beat music that had turned his gut into knots in his recent sessions in Shebel's rooms.

They couldn't see with his eyes the picture his mind had dug up out of its protective mire: the picture of a dark eleven year-old boy perched on the foot of the bed in his underpants.

They couldn't feel with his gut the horror of watching the boy, terror in his eyes at the lusting hover of three men. The disgust at their inappropriate state of dress — actually of undress. One leaning against the wardrobe in white shorts, an orange tennis shirt over his bare shoulder. A second in only a wrinkled Hawaiian shirt down to the top of bare thighs, his genitals peeping from the hem. A third, a big man, sitting legs-crossed in a chair in a white singlet tucked into flannelet undies, beer in hand, cans on ice in a baby bath nearby.

Then the shock of a fourth man sidling in from the

Streaker

left, almost filling the field of view. A spare framed man draped in a black silk kimono with a Japanese ideogram on its back. A Commodore's cap on his head, which he removed and flopped onto the table where it merged with the real-time version the two woman *could* see unsegued with any dream-state. On the cap's front, "TOP COX" embroidered over an anchor.

Koh and Schebel were alarmed at the sudden change that swept over Traeger's face. They had no idea what his subconscious was playing before his eyes. The spare-framed man advancing toward the bed, then slowly, with obvious relish, dropping his robe off his shoulders ...

The two woman shuddered at the piteous wail that came out of their "patient".

They couldn't know that *he* heard it, not as a sound from his own lips, but rather the wail of fear from an eleven-year-old boy.

25: Break-ins

"Around the back. Get him in here where he can sit down." Shouted.

Cassandra Koh was at the back porch. She smashed her torch into the glass panel of the sidelight. Put her hand in and unlatched the door. Swung it open.

\#

The room was dark. Torch light flickered from beyond the doorway.

"No. Don't. I want to see." An off-stage question and an off-stage response.

"There are plenty of places you can rest and recover without going in there."

Traeger appeared in the doorway, Schebel 's hand on his arm. He wrenched away. Flipped the light switch on. Stomped into the room. Crossed to the bed. Schebel followed. Hovered, concerned.

"Those cockroaches. Filthy low-life cockroaches."

"You must give it time. It has all come back in too much of a rush."

Koh entered the room. She clutched a handful of photos.

His subconscious spilt its guts.

"Everything. Me in Mackerel fishing when Hetty's

Streaker

family arrived in the water taxi that week. Felicity, the driver, making friends with us. Hetty pestering me to teach her to fish. The night she sneaked out to check crab pots with me. On the way, me seeing the light on in a place I'd never seen lit before. That awful music. The hat. Me sneaking up to peek in at those ... those ... men abusing that poor kid. Knowing that what they were doing was wrong … dead wrong … but hearing my mother saying men were like that and me hating that I might be like that too. My mind so muddled, all I could do was send Hetty home and get somewhere fast to drink myself into a stupor."

Koh crossed to the bed and laid out a three-by-four array of photographs of young boys in various stages of undress.

"Not just the one poor kid, Tiger. I found these in a kitchen drawer."

Traeger scowled down at the array, his fists clenching.

"Those low-life scum. If only I knew who ... And where I could get my hands on them."

The scrape of boots on timber flooring had the trio spinning to face the door. Two men suddenly appeared in the doorway. Both held revolvers. Both pistols were raised, hammers back. And pointed at the occupants of the room.

"Look no further, Denny boy."

Traeger gasped. The tall man with a man-bun he recognised from his memory flood of that terrible night he had witnessed horrors from the window of this very room. But that was not what had delivered the shock. It was the smaller man in the lead. The man in the kimono on that same night. The man he now recognised as his boss.

Senator Arthur Candy.

Who spoke sharply before anyone could react.

Robin duMerrick

"Nuh-uh, Sergeant Koh, letting that hand stray to your bag would not, I assure you, be a good idea."

Traeger's shock gave way to fury.

"Now it makes sense. How hard you lobbied to head that subcommittee. The moment I set eyes on the photos Koh found, I thought I recognised some of the refugee kids you drool over at your desk. You're using the so-called policy review to set up a foster home scheme to groom the youngsters for your filthy ring of pederast pals."

"And loving it. But what I want to know is how you found our little kiddy love nest. I was assured the Fallon and Khalib investigations were going nowhere. Care to answer that, Sergeant Koh, mm?"

Koh took half a step forward. Her grin was grim, but even so, a grin. Bravado? Or was she really as tough as she appeared. Certainly there was no quaver in her voice. She patted her bag.

"Too easy. If you weren't so anal about me reaching into my bag, I'd show you the list I downloaded just an hour ago of Mackerel rate payers of seventeen years ago. I cross-checked that with the list of property owners interviewed by the case detectives. That list was one short. The name leapt out at me."

"Mine. Of course. Suggesting the lead detective needed to keep me out of it."

"Not to mention who, years later, pulled me off the Dimitriou case the moment I put *you* on the list of suspects for Hetty Dimitriou's gassing."

"Mm." Then voice raised. "Hear that, Juric? No point in skulking out there when you've been thoroughly made."

Candy and his companion stepped aside to let enter a blubbering individual whom Traeger recognised as the big man from that infamous night but whom Koh recognised in quite another context. One that had her

120

Streaker

adding her gasps to Traeger's.

"Stefan fucking Juric. Oh, what a shit."

"I should've had you gassed along with that damned left-wing troublemaker, Dimitriou."

"What, you don't do your own dirty work, Juric? So which of you drowned Felicity Fallon when you found her looking in on your kid-abusing session that night?"

Candy appeared willing to be amused.

"You figure that how?"

"Fibres off rope used by locals on their cray pots were found on the water taxi's propeller. But no knife to cut away a tangle. She had to've paddled into Mackerel for help. Got herself drowned instead."

Juric growled.

"Too damned smart for your own good, Koh. Always were."

Candy waved it off. Crossed to the table by the window to lift off the "TOP COX" hat and firm it onto his head.

"Quite. So what are we to do with our detractors."

The tall guy in the man-bun didn't hesitate.

"Same as we did with the Fallon broad, sir."

"You think we can pull that off, Vance?"

Robin duMerrick

26: Death ride

Sappho nudged ahead under twin engines barely over idle. The dark shore slid by on the port side. The flybridge cruiser was level with where the beach gave way to the rocks of the headland.

Vance, the tall slim Canadian with his hair in a man-bun, exited the foc's'le with two wood-handled hanks of rope. In his stride through the cabin, he had to squeeze past Arthur Candy standing beside a fat man at the inside helm.

In the cockpit, Stefan Juric had words for Vance as he stepped aside for the Canadian to pass. Juric had a .308 rifle clamped across his chest.

"How do you propose we drown three people at once? They're not puppies out of a litter, you know, Vance."

"Too easy. We use water-ski tow ropes to drag them behind us by the feet. I give them five minutes."

Vance hugged the port side of the cockpit to stay well clear of the captives, who had been forced to sit along the other gunwale. First the lady cop, then next to her the older chick with the figure, and finally Candy's press guy.

The Canadian went right aft. Laid the hanks of rope

122

Streaker

on the transom. Teased them apart where they had tangled. Frowned.

"Should be three. I know there was three."

He turned, retraced his steps into the cabin and ducked down into the foc's'le again.

Traeger feigned a coughing fit into his right hand. His doubling up brought him close enough to Schebel's ear to risk a whisper.

"Distract him."

Juric straightened, thrusting out his big-bore firearm.

"Did someone say something? I said for you all to shut up."

Shebel was quick to speak.

"He said for us to pray."

"Huh. You won't be doing much of that where you lot are going."

"In which case, I shall do what I have longed to do since I met Cassie, and to hell with you."

Koh turned in surprise at the use of her name. Schebel sandwiched the cop's head between her hands and lip-locked Koh hard.

Which brain-locked Juric momentarily.

"Huh? Hey ..."

Long enough for him to react late to Traeger's fluid move. His dash for the opposite gunwale, where he swept the water-ski towlines off the stern on the way to diving over the side.

Traeger went deep, fast. The towlines sank slower at first, but suddenly swifter when gulped into the props. In the blink of an eye, the tangle enmeshed the twin screws, which struggled and jammed and the engines stalled. Their idling quit.

Underwater, Traeger shrugged off his shirt, kicked off his pants and shoes and breast-stroked for the shore.

123

On deck, Arthur Candy was livid in his rush from the cabin at the melee.

"*Oaf. Give you one thing to do and you fuck it.* He surfaces, shoot him. Rollo, work that searchlight. Vance, lock these women below ..."

Candy broke out the paddles. Vance herded Koh and Schebel through the cabin into the foc's'le.

"… then get back here to help me get us back to the damn beach."

Underwater, Traeger swam on, no trace of panic in his steady stroke. As an orphan of Pittwater, he was at home on the water or in it. Or under it.

Streaker

27: His turf

The sea lapped on dark rocks. Near offshore, a lit Sappho crawled back toward the beach silently, long paddles working hard off each gunwale in the tiring hands of one tall man and one shorter man.

Sappho's spotlight swept the rocks, lingered, moved on.

Among the rocks, Traeger's head emerged from the water just to the eyes. His mouth ventured out, blew air. Cautiously, his body slithered onto the rocks. He rose to a crouch, moved off.

He got to where the rocks ended and beach began. The beam swept back. He flattened. The beam moved on. He straightened again and ran for the cover of the tussock.

He peeked past his cover at Sappho halfway back to the beach. He turned, kept low, scuttled off. His heart rate up but under control. This was his turf. If they were determined to play, it would be on his terms.

#

The shack was on the beach, backed by sand dunes. Its timbers grey with age. It had a narrow veranda at front. By the door, a faded sticker showed a giant grouper with "I DIVED THE FAMOUS COD HOLE"

Robin duMerrick

painted in red with a scraggy brush.

Voices came across the water from a distant Sappho, its paddlers cursing as they struggled to make way.

Close by the shack, floorboards groaned. A piece of driftwood in a pair of hands smashed the glass window by the door. The wood clubbed away the jagged edges. A hand reached in and the door squeaked open.

Inside the shack, Traeger reminded himself of its layout. Unchanged from oftentimes he'd been with Swampy dropping in on his mate Squidgy McDowel to share their catch of mackerel and a bottle of overproof Bundy.

Sparely furnished. Wood table, canvas chairs, bed litter. Tin wash basin. Metho stove. Shelf of foodstuffs. Camp food safe hanging from a ceiling hook.

Traeger moved to the left rear of the shack. He drew back a curtain hanging across the corner. A wetsuit was on a hanger. A dive mask on a peg. Swimfins on the floor.

He reached in for what he knew would be there. A speargun and an extra spear. He hesitated before snatching out a fishing gaff with a fist-sized gaff hook. Finally shouldered a coil of hemp rope.

He hustled out the door.

The floorboards groaned again.

Streaker

28: The hunt

The Sappho nosed onto the beach. Vance leapt over the side. He turned the vessel around, stern to beach, so he could get at the propellers with knife in hand.

Candy jumped out. The fat man and the big cop crowded the near gunwale, tilting down the starboard side.

"Vance, leave that to Rollo. You come with me."

The fat man climbed over the side. Exchanged pistol for knife and began sawing at the tangle around the props.

A distant thud had Rollo cocking his chubby head.

"What was that?"

"What was what?"

The faint thud repeated before Candy got an answer.

"That."

"I think I heard it too." This from the Canadian.

"If it was Traeger, it means he didn't drown. So he needs hunting down." Candy directed traffic. "Juric, you stand guard on those women and don't fuck up this time."

Juric put the .308 across his chest like a sentry.

Candy and Vance crossed the sand. Melted into the

shadows.

Streaker

29: In the balance

Traeger had stored away, in the back of his mind, the image of the old 30 foot deep-keeler he and Koh had passed on their way to the cottage where she'd said the Dimitrous had holidayed seventeen years ago.

Almost by instinct he sought it now. Still as he remembered it, sitting upright on a hardstand between two cottages, propped by three 4x2 timbers under the near gunwale. A 44-gal drum, rusty paint scrapers on it, near the boat's seaward-pointing bow.

The only change to the location was to the street lamp beside the walking track edging the beach. Then, in daylight, it was unlit. Now, it threw down a broad cone of light onto the path, the beach and the space between the boat and the northernmost cottage.

Traeger was in this space now, close to the yacht. He had picked up a heavy billet of wood left over from chocking the boat level under the keel's stern and bow rise. He used it to hammer aside the nearest of the props. The yacht creaked. He hammered aside the far prop. He backed away at the louder creak. But the yacht stayed put.

He tied a clove hitch in his rope around the central and final prop, right up as high as he could reach.

He payed out the rope as far as the 44-gallon drum. Rolled the drum, still paying out rope, to the foot of the street light pole. The weapons he had gained from the shack lay where he had left them right by the pole.

He cast the rest of the rope over the steel arm suspending the lamp. Made a large rope loop with a bowline up high. Took up the slack.

He nodded satisfaction, gathered weapons and loop and crouched out of sight behind the drum.

Streaker

30: Shafted

Candy's voice was low into Vance's ear as they went into a huddle against a cottage on the beach, pistols in hand: six-shooters with suppressors.

"If he got to shore, he couldn't have made it this far south. But he could be heading inland, trying to skirt us. Let's spread out. You go inland as far as the gully and sweep north. I'll check these cottages all the way to the rocks.

They faded into the shadows.

\#

Alone, Candy moved stealthily, gun at the ready. He eased onto the veranda of a weekender, tried the door. It was locked.

He dropped off the veranda and headed for the next. As he went, he cautiously peered into the gap between buildings.

Ahead, the track in front of the cottages was lit better than in most places. He saw a 44-gallon drum ahead by a light standard, dismissed it and moved on. Hugged the corner as he squinted down the gap at a yacht propped upright on a hardstand.

Down the near narrow side of the yacht the gap was dark.

He allowed his eyes to adjust before moving on. He scanned the wider lit side. He was moving on past the gap when the last thing he expected happened nearby. A voice. A casual voice.

"Only big boys to play with here, Arthur."

Candy spun, gun raised to Traeger leaning on the fuel drum, right fingers over the far drum edge, apparently unarmed. Seeing this, Candy relaxed.

The voice continued. Conversationally.

"Who would've thought? A rock-spider. How many of those billeted-out refugee boys have you abused and discarded like worn-out shoes over the years?"

Candy stifled the urge to curse aloud. Forced himself to relax and used a slow-spreading grin to show just how in-control he was despite the shock he must've felt. He drawled his diagnosis of the situation to add to the impression. Let the pistol sit loose in a palm-up gesture of a dismissive hand.

"Pity to go to all this trouble to escape my clutches for nothing. I would, of course, shoot you on the spot. However, I would really rather go with the accidental drowning option." Chatty. But then shouting loud enough to bounce off the escarpment.

"*Vance, get here. By the light. I've got him.*"

Before going back to chatty.

"Turn around, Denny, and head back toward the jetty. You know the way. I'll be right behind you."

Candy moved forward, overconfident.

"No, Arthur, I think I'd rather ... do *this*."

Like a conjuring trick, the speargun appeared from behind the drum in Traeger's hand. Candy's eyes went wide as he brought up his gun too late, the spear zinging then making a thunk sound as it buried itself deep in under his ribs.

Reflexes loosed a round from Candy's gun. Traeger ducked behind the drum as the the bullet twanged into

Streaker

the steel. He stayed low and got busy behind cover. Candy staggered. Another loose round ricocheted off the steel. Traeger popped up with his second spear loaded in the speargun.

He was about to fire but held off. Candy was wobbly, his eyes glazing.

The senator pitched forward, doubling onto the drum.

Robin duMerrick

31 : Nowhere to run

Vance stood at the inland end of a gap between cottages where a yacht was propped upright on a hardstand.

A light shone on a pole at the other end of the gap.

He looked seaward along the yacht's flank, moving cautiously forward, gun held at the ready.

He'd heard shots. *After* he'd heard his boss shout for him to head for the light.

"Boss?"

He stopped, gob-smacked, halfway to the end in the shadow of the yacht towering over him. Ahead, Traeger stood on the top of a drum in full view under a light, grinning like a fool. Draped over the drum, a man, a steel shaft jutting from him. Candy, his boss.

Traeger had his right foot in a stirrup of rope. Vance's eye followed the rope up over the arm of the street light, back over his head to the only timber propping up the yacht.

His eyes widened. Traeger, grin spreading, stepped off the drum. The rope twanged tight. The end of the prop jerked free. The yacht toppled. Vance started running. The sky closed over him as the yacht descended.

Streaker

The scream echoed into every corner of Mackerel Beach.

32: Hooked

The fat man, Rollo, was up to his thighs in the sea. He muttered as he hacked away at the rope tangled around Sappho's props.

He had heard the scream. Thought that at least Candy and Vance had put an end to it all somehow.

That and his concentration on his task lulled him into a less-than-vigilant state. So he wasn't aware of the hook of a gaff that reached out from behind.

It encircled his neck as if made for it. A tight fit which, when jerked back before he knew it, choked off his muffled cry.

His head was pulled back, down and into the water despite his struggles.

Bubbles surfaced in bursts from where he had been dragged under. The bursts came less often. Stopped.

Streaker

33: Anesti

Stefan Juric sat stiff upright on the transom, facing Sappho's bow, the .308 high across his chest.

"How's it going, Rollo? Winning?"

And when there was no answer.

"Did you hear that bellow? Sounds like they got 'im, what?"

Rollo, he knew, wasn't very good at doing two things at once. Even as simple as cutting and talking. A lazy, uncoordinated fat man, really.

The big boss cop was content to wait. It was a pleasant night and it looked like their problems were solved. He tilted his head back to study the stars coming out now the clouds were clearing.

He didn't hear anything above the gentle lap of the water behind him around Sappho's motors. So he was oblivious of the shadow-form barely disturbing the water as it moved into the space right up to the transom. The form eased from the sea until it was upright just behind him.

The tip of a speargun spear moved steadily closer to the back of Juric's head. He prattled on.

"It was Vance's fault, you know, leaving the towropes where the arsehole could get to them."

Robin duMerrick

He suddenly stiffened, simultaneously hearing the voice and feeling something sharp dig into the soft cleft at the back of his skull. A voice spoken quick and deadly.

"Move and you're a dead man."

"Wha ...?"

Fear froze even Juric's vocal chords.

"That's the pointy end of a speargun you can feel. My trigger finger already has the tremors. A flinch could be all it takes for your head to be first meat on a souflaki skewer." A beat let that sink in. Then: "Slowly now, move both hands onto the barrel of your rifle and grip it."

Juric obeyed, clamping his anal sphincter against his stomach turning to water.

"Now put the butt on the gunwale and push with both hands ... that's it ... until it's past its point of balance. Good, now let go."

The rifle splashed over the side.

"Now stand and move toward the cabin. Don't look around. I assure you I'll be right behind you."

Juric moved. Traeger eased over the transom.

"On to the foc's'le. Open it."

Juric unsnicked the foc's'le door and slid it back. The heads of Koh and Schebel appeared.

"Hello, girls. It's only me. As soon as I sit this buffoon down, come on out."

Traeger gestured Juric into the helmsman's seat. He swivelled the seat to face the corner. He slid the seat forward on its tracks to jam the big man in.

Koh and Schebel emerged. They edged past Juric.

The two women said it in unison.

"Are you all right? "

"Not too bad for an ex-nutter."

Schebel's brow showed concern.

"We heard shots. Screams."

Streaker

"An alto tenor of our acquaintance. I can't reach such high notes."

"How ever did you ...?"

Koh was flippant.

"What took you so long?"

"Cassie, the man has just ..."

"It's okay. She has a James Bond fixation."

Koh snorted.

"More to the point is what we do now. We have to get to where we can call up the troops."

Traeger mulled that over. Suddenly thrust the speargun into Koh's hands.

"Keep the naughty boy in his corner. I'm going to see if I can finish what the chubby chum started and clear the props."

He headed for the stern but turned back at Koh's query.

"What happened to him anyway?"

"You don't want to know."

Traeger expected any possible rejoinder could only come from one of Sappho's three occupants. It didn't. The surprise growl behind him came from out in the night. A cornered panther growl laced with pain.

"I ... *already* ... know."

Traeger spun at the voice. Scowled at Arthur Candy between the motors at the stern. Gun in his right hand. His left hand gripped the shaft of the spear still in his gut. He looked like death.

"And you're not going anywhere. Drop that speargun, young lady. *Now!* I'm allergic to them. They make me break out in a rash" Then screaming at her tardiness. "*Do it!*"

Koh let the speargun fall onto the cushioned seat next to her and showed her hands. Juric struggled in a futile effort to get out from behind the helmsman's seat.

Robin duMerrick

Traeger hissed his regret.

"I should've put the second spear in you to make the rash permanent."

"Ah, not necessary I assure you, dear boy. You see, what with half crawling here ... with this piece of steel in me, I figure I have ... at best half an hour before ... it all catches up with me."

Candy's voice was full of catches and breaks as the pains hit him deep down.

He almost doubled. Traeger saw his chance and took his first step to rush the older man.

But Candy recovered with a start and waved the gun in grim warning.

Juric continued to struggle, but was jammed in by his own beer gut.

"Just enough time for me to watch you suffer with your own belly full of death ... Lead rather than steel death, of course ... You never know, you might even last ... as long as I do. Only I will make sure I place the lead ... where the pain will be far worse ... than my steel."

Candy levelled his six-shooter. His thumb pulled back the hammer. The magazine revolved. There was nothing any of those aboard Sappho could do.

A double-barrelled roar erupted in their ears at the same moment Candy's head shredded in a scatter of bone, flesh and brains. His headless body crumpled out of sight behind Sappho's transom, his Commodore's hat lobbing, against the odds, on the top of the starboard engine cowling, its "TOP COX" emblem facing them, tattered and bloody.

Schebel's hand went to her mouth. Koh grabbed up the speargun and gestured Juric to cease trying to extricate himself from behind the helm. Traeger rushed to the stern, baffled. He scanned the darkness toward where the sound had come from. From the north.

Streaker

His face lit up.

"Swampy, you old skinflint. What were you doing? Trolling the shallows for tiddlers?"

Swampy stood up to his knees in the water three paces away, ejecting empty shells from both barrels of his coach gun.

His response was matter-of-fact.

"Came in up the beach under 'lectric power ..." He thumbed over his shoulder at his riverboat back where the creek cut a shallow trench across the sand. "... when I heard the shots. Reckoned it might be them shitters at it again what shot up my stretch of water. Guess they won't do that again in a hurry, young fella. What?"

"You could be right, Swampy. You could be right. Now what do you say about giving us all a lift over to Palm Beach to fetch the coppers?" He gestured at Juric. "Oh, but there'll be one more on board than when we came."

Swampy waved his shotgun.

"If that's one of them shitters, you'd better tell 'im to sit tight or me shotty'll have something to say."

"I'll make sure he knows it, old friend."

34: Surprise party

They had just pulled up. The traffic had eased from peak hour long ago and the theatre crowd wasn't yet released from shows in the city.

"I don't really think I'm up to it."

Shebel switched off and turned a little sideways to respond to her passenger.

"I told you. It is not a good idea for you to be alone right now."

"Giving police statements is draining, specially explaining away so many dead bodies."

"It was draining on everyone. Don't fret about it. The only one left facing committal is that horrible Juric man. Now come on."

She started to get out. He barely stirred.

"Who'll be there?"

"No one you don't know. Come on. Doctor's orders."

She climbed out. He followed. Reluctantly.

#

The pub was far from full. Just the same, the chatter forced conversation up a level in pitch.

Traeger trailed Schebel into the lounge bar. Propped, mouth open, when he saw who was at the two tables

Streaker

that had been put end-to-end in the near corner as far away from the long bar as possible.

Eight of the chairs around the two tables were already occupied. The occupants all turned to the arrival of the newcomers.

The compact man in his fifties with bushy eyebrows and tousled grey-tinged hair who rose from his chair at the head of the table was Traeger's most recent acquaintance. A superintendent of detectives who had been present when he gave his statement earlier this evening. Trumble, who was first to speak now.

"Ah, the man of the hour at last. Raise your glasses to the man who, in one night, solved the Fallon, Khalib and Dimitriou murders, which had baffled police over more than a decade and a half, and put away a bad cop into the bargain."

Everyone clinked glasses. Traeger looked at Schebel. Her smile told him she was in on this surprise.

Koh, on the other side, stood, smiled and proffered a glass of wine. Traeger let Schebel push him to the empty chair between Koh and Trumble and took the chair beside Koh herself.

But Traeger wouldn't sit. His puckered face suggested he was puzzled by the presence of some at what was clearly a celebration meant for him.

Leith Fallon, he supposed, could have been wanting to meet the man who had caught the killers of his mother. But what was Fran Mazzotti, the lady water taxi driver doing here? And Yodel, whose only connection to the evening's events was that he happened to be driving a ferry when Traeger had seen a streaker he had mistaken for a woman dead seventeen years. And the old couple, John and Clara Wentworth, who had bought Fallon Hall and put him on the trail of Leith Fallon at the beginning of it all.

Trumble hastened to relieve the puzzlement.

143

Robin duMerrick

"Oh, of course, how rude of me not to introduce some you only think you know. First Detective Sergeant Ted Gaston, who you know as Leith Fallon.

Gaston/Fallon stood. Thrust out a hand. Traeger took it, his face taut with confusion.

"You're not Felicity Fallon's son?".

"Nah. The real Leith Fallon is doing time for ... ha, get this ... impersonating an officer."

"Quite." Trumble gestured further along the table. "Moving on. Constable Fran Mazzotti you saw a lot more of than just driving a water taxi."

Mazzotti gave him a cheeky grin, not the least bashful.

"A lot more. In fact, coming out of the water in Elvina Bay, all there is to see of me."

She picked up a folded paper on the table in front of her. She unfolded it. Slapped it down. He recognised it as a printout of the still he took of her climbing the garden to Fallon Hall, nude. The copy Koh had ordered the police clerk to add to her casefile. Of the printout Traeger had likened to the bare-backed Mazzotti sunning herself on their arrival at Mackerel just a day ago.

Yodel piped in with a psuedo-gripe.

"Which I missed out on, darn it. Strictly eyes front, they said I had to be, every time the Streaker streaked with me at the wheel."

Swampy's eyes went wide as he leant way over to stare down at the printout.

"I never got me a job like that when *I* was a young'un. Where do I sign on?"

Traeger was staring at it too. When it dawned.

"*You* were the skinny-dipper? My Streaker? And the mother in an obviously fake Fallon family shot? All a set-up? Even *that*?

John Wentworth was clearly delighted to join in the

Streaker

revelations.

"To spur you to pursue your own line of enquiry."

As did Clara Wentworth—if that was her real name.

"On Dr Schebel's say-so that you had to be the one to shed light on your own problem or you might bury it forever."

"And in the process, hopefully solving a seventeen year old cold case."

"You two aren't the Wentworths, owners of Fallon Hall, at all?"

Countered quickly by Trumble.

"Oh, they're the Wentworths right enough. But only owners for a day of a temporarily-plaqued Fallon Hall. Say hello to John Wentworth, Forensics's handwriting expert and his real-life wife, whose name is indeed Clara. They were a fiction to get you going on your own epic journey of discovery."

Koh joined in.

"... from mystery swimmer ... via the Wentworths ... to Ted Gaston as Leith Fallon ... to me ... with prodding from Laura ... ultimately to your personal house of horrors."

Traeger flopped into his chair, grappling with it.

Laura Schebel laid a hand over his.

"I'm sorry, Denny. It was a cruel ruse, but as you can see, it worked. For everyone."

The group went quiet watching his face, not sure what his reaction might be. He looked dark.

When he spoke, his face was stern as his eyes swept from one to the other around the table, sparing none.

"A sadder bunch of ham actors I've yet to come across in my life. But ..." He let it hang, and it was as if everyone at the table held their breath at the same time. Then he suddenly grinned. "... you sure had me fooled." He raised his glass. "Here's to your conniving

145

Robin duMerrick

... with thanks for giving me back my past and shaking off some serious demons."

He drank. The table relaxed. Laughter and toasting followed.

Schebel was the only one who watched, face stern, as Traeger bent to whisper into Koh's ear.

"As for you, lady cop, I don't know that I can ever forget what you thought I was capable of."

Koh tried to put her hand on his.

"Sorry, Tiger. Forgive? Please?"

But he pulled his hand from under hers. Schebel looked on, unhappy with the interplay, her eyes longingly on Koh.

#

The crowd in the lounge bar had grown. The volume of the chatter was now at a level that all but discouraged conversation.

At the long table made up of two tables butted together, heads of neighbours came together to exchange chat. Before them were half full glasses, empties, plates of eats and nibbles scattered by careless finger-dips.

The men had removed their coats. Trumble had taken off his tie. Twos and threes were in chat groups. Trumble and Traeger alone were unengaged.

Trumble wore a silly paternal grin as he looked over his flock having a good time. Traeger looked weary.

With Koh and Schebel turned to each other in conversation, Traeger seized the moment. Slid his chair back. Stood. Bent to Trumble, who nodded. They shook hands. Traeger left.

Streaker

35: Strollers

Traeger paused under the street light outside the pub. Nearby, a rubbish bin in a pebble fronted enclosure overflowed with trash. He looked at the sky. A cold front was coming. He shrugged his shoulders and zipped up his jacket.

He was about to step away when a voice stopped him.

"Hey, wait up, Tiger."

He turned to see Koh hurry from the pub entrance, her bag over her shoulder. She clutched a folded sheet of paper.

"You left this behind."

He watched her cover the distance between them. She thrust the paper at him. He took it in his left hand. He knew what it was but unfolded it just the same. The printout that Mazzotti tabled in the pub not more than two hours ago.

"I thought you might keep it to look at from time to time. You know, to remind you of the one that got away. In the skinny and everything."

He studied it a long time. Then he lifted his head and studied Koh unsmiling for so long she began to fidget.

"What?"

"You thought the nude thing was something I would treasure?"

"Well, you have to admit, she has something more than a boyish figure."

He continued to study her as he slowly extended his left arm toward the rubbish bin.

"You know what I think?"

She took half a step closer. She looked anxious, as if his next words might be the most important she had heard in her life.

"What?"

He dropped the printout onto the trash in the bin before answering.

"I think that, as fish go, I can do better. Or as cops go for that matter. What do you think?"

Koh's faces broke into a grin, washing away most of the anxiety.

"I think you're right." Then more confidently. "In fact, Tiger, I'm sure of it."

She took the half step needed to clutch his left arm by the elbow he extended and hooked to accommodate her.

They walked off arm-in-arm down the street.

They were in the distance when a breeze stirred the trash in the bin. The sheet of paper fluttered. Whipped from the bin and, face up, slithered and spun along the pavement. Up close showing—to anyone who cared to look—the image of the Streaker.

Murders and psych hell in Sydney's Pittwater

Bomb threat in Sydney's Darling Harbour

Shop for these duMer creatives at www.robindumerrick.com

Cruise ship dogged by the Black Dog

Witch-work catches thief of Sir Don's baggy green

Smuggling on the Great Barrier Reef

Murders in SA's Port Lincoln

Insert a mate's name into each ditty, shoot and text to her or him

Cyclone and cyclonic romance in the Whitsunday Islands

CPSIA information can be obtained
at www.ICGtesting.com
Printed in the USA
BVHW060404260321
603416BV00003B/296